Cotton Factory Shorts

Cotton Factory Shorts
Fiction from
The Cotton Factory Times

Ethel Carnie Holdsworth

with Introductions by
Jackie Thompson
and Jennifer Reid

Kennedy & Boyd
an imprint of
Zeticula Ltd
Unit 13,
196 Rose Street,
Edinburgh,
EH2 4AT.

http://www.kennedyandboyd.co.uk
admin@kennedyandboyd.co.uk

First published in *The Cotton Factory Times* 1906-1920

This edition © Zeticula Ltd 2024

Ethel Carnie Holdsworth published under her maiden name (Ethel Carnie) and with various versions of her married name.

Front cover image: Ethel Carnie Holdsworth.
Reproduced with kind permission from Helen Brown.

Photographs by Frank Shorrock © Jackie Thompson 2024

ISBN 978-1-84921-247-2

Publisher's Note

"The Cotton Factory Times" was first published on Friday, January 16, 1885 by William Glover at 1 Warren Street, Cross Street, Manchester, and printed by J. Andrew & Co, Ashton-under-Lyne.

"The Yorkshire Factory Times" was still publishing in April 1926, owned by Senior & Co, Heckmondwike.

Letterpress printing, with each character set by hand, was a skilled and time-consuming task. Hundreds of newspapers gave employment to many men, and speed and accuracy were qualities to be sought. In the 1921 Census, there are five compositors listed as working for J. Andrew, in Ashton-under-Lyne.

Local newspapers would have little time for proof-reading, and Holdsworth was unlikely to have present. She would had no opportunity to check for simple errors like punctuation, transcription errors, or her own spelling mistakes.

Albion Mill, Blackburn, 1960s.
Photograph by Frank Shorrock

Contents

Blackburn at dusk, 1960s. Photograph by Frank Shorrock

Introduction

My introduction to Ethel Carnie Holdsworth came late via the Working-Class Movement Library in Salford. I read her first novel, *Miss Nobody,* in 2019, which is ridiculous really, because you would've thought Ethel's books would be studied in every school in Blackburn. Reading it made me wonder, if I'd had Ethel as inspiration from a young age would I have come to writing sooner than I did. I think the answer is, yes. I identified with everything in *Miss Nobody.* Especially how similar I felt to Ethel the narrator and the main character, Carrie Brown. I couldn't believe that someone who existed 110 years ago thinks exactly like me. We have the same anger towards injustice, the same weakness for the underdog, the same contempt for authority, the same struggle for independence, the same tendency to turn disadvantage to advantage, the same need to right, wrongs, the same desire to see a bully get their comeuppance, all of which are recurring themes that run through Ethel's stories; but most of all we have the same love and pride in 'our lot', the working class.

I started mentally ticking off in my head any similarities I discovered about me and Ethel. We're both from Blackburn (well, Ethel's from Great Harwood actually, but they're so similar that I feel ok claiming Ethel as one of my own), we're both working class, we're both writers, we both moved to Manchester, we both wrote for children, we both progressed in our chosen careers by having middle class patrons, we both worked in a mill. (I worked in a mill in the 1990s, the women weren't allowed to wear trousers, so I wore culottes most days to smash the system. Whilst working there as a sales ledger clerk I developed a system for reconciling invoices and statements which involved putting the statements in the bin if they didn't balance second time), We both got sacked from jobs and my late mum Marilyn's middle name is Ethel.

I've seen mostly academic articles written about Ethel and the times she lived in, in relation to feminism, politics and class but I'm not at all academic despite my six GCSEs. Neither politics nor feminism was discussed in our house growing up. Apart from when I'd kick off at my mum and dad about why it was always me being asked to make a brew or switch the light on and not my brother.

My interest in Ethel is personal rather than academic. I want to know how she felt being a working-class woman from Blackburn who obviously thought and behaved differently to most women from her background at the time. I've got so many questions about Ethel's life. Was her choice to be a writer accepted by her family and friends? Did she feel accepted rather than understood by the people around her? Did her workmates in the mill treat her like she thought she was better than everyone else for wanting to be a writer or were they proud of her? How did she reconcile needing middle-class patrons to do what she loved? Did she feel any imposter syndrome when she was writing?

It seems from Ethel's writing that she didn't feel inadequate because of her working-class roots, the opposite in fact. All her writing is about giving a voice to working class people and writing unapologetically in her voice, to be read by people with the same voice, who cares if the literary world gets it. I think the same. My writing style might not be for everyone, unless you love tenses changing on a penny and really long sentences, but it's how I write as a self-taught script writer. I can't write any other way. Ethel's defiant spirit has spurred me on every time my imposter syndrome showed up whilst writing this introduction. I put Ethel Carnie Holdsworth (and me and Jennifer), in the 'working class till I die' category.

Regardless of money, success or position in society, Ethel carried on writing stories dealing with inequalities relating to class and celebrating working class grit and humour. Reading Ethel's stories made me love being a working-class woman from Blackburn. I got a feeling of pride when I understood the parts written in dialect without having to look online for the meaning. I loved that you had to be from Lancashire to get it. I know the characters in her stories because I grew up with them and worked with them. The good and the bad. The 'women-hating' female bosses, the jealous sisters of boyfriends, the emotionally repressed men.

I've had the same soul-destroying conversations and unsolicited advice to "find yourself a rich fella". This advice was first given to me in the 1980s and still crops up occasionally. The seeming lack of belief in me and my abilities had a profound effect on me from a young age. It forced me to back myself and want more options than to marry well, or work in a bank. Which seemed to be the only way to better your life if you were a working-class woman who didn't go to university. The world Ethel Carnie wrote from doesn't seem that different to the world we're living in. The patriarchy still rules, women who want to live independently are vilified and treated like oddballs. The fight for workers' rights feels the same and the divide between rich and poor feels the same.

Whenever I read Ethel's stories, I find myself wanting to know what drove her to write those stories. I imagine that she would've been seen as a non-conformist in Blackburn in the 1900s not just because of Ethel's radical political views (that probably got her the sack from *The Woman Worker* magazine) but mostly because of the plight of Carrie Brown in *Miss Nobody*. I know Carrie Brown is a fictional character, but I see Carrie and Ethel as the same person, fighting for the same things. Fighting the pressure to do what society expected of them as women. Wanting to live their lives according to their own morals and rules, not anybody else's.

Did Ethel write stories set in familiar domestic settings with familiar characters to be able to make her views understood by an audience who might have thought her views were odd? Or was she just writing about what she knew? Did she write stories set in workplaces and published in publications like the *Cotton Factory Times* as escapism for the workers? Or was it an attempt to rally people to join together to change their dire working conditions? If the latter was Ethel's plan, I think it worked because I know that Lancashire women cotton workers were some of the highest paid and most unionised in Britain; another reason I feel proud to be a working class woman from Blackburn. I feel proud to come from strong Lancashire women like Ethel, and my great grandma, Elizabeth who was working in the mills in Blackburn, aged 13 and would've been involved in the fight for better conditions.

I'm conflicted when I talk about feeling proud. I don't want to romanticise pride because I see pride as positive and negative when I think about Blackburn. Pride stops people talking about how they feel. Keeping things in is seen as being strong and resilient. There's pride in resilience but I have a problem with how much the word resilience is used in relation to working class people. It's more about the withstanding difficulties definition of resilience than the bouncing back or recovery from those difficulties. How much can you take? We're brought up to be resilient in Blackburn because I think, historically, the expectation was that things would get worse, not better, so there's no point worrying because you're going to have something to worry about, forever.

I'm convinced this fatalistic belief is why humour is so prevalent in Blackburn. I recently made the connection between this belief and a funny comment my dad has always said whenever someone says "sorry" to him. Without a beat he says, "you will be". I see the cautionary tale in the comment, if you think you're sorry now, just wait. Which could be translated as stop wasting your time being sorry, stop worrying. I learned the hard way that not everyone gets that joke when I was called into my boss's office to discuss my 'threatening behaviour' reported by a colleague, who, in my defence, did say "sorry" a lot. I like to think that the 'threatening behaviour' I picked up from my dad helped my colleague stop saying "sorry" unnecessarily. I was totally baffled that they couldn't see the humour in someone saying "you will be" at them 20 times a day.

Lancashire humour can be seen as harsh or cruel sometimes by people who aren't from there. I know it's got me into trouble loads of times over the years. I had to develop a thick skin growing up in my family because our comedy chops were being tested from a young age. I came late to sarcasm and wit compared to my brother; I think I was about 4 before I properly got it. The humour in our house was never intentionally mean, the only time the humour was harsh was if it was ridiculing an authority figure, who probably deserved it, or bringing a show off down a peg or two, but those kind of jokes were rare. The intention was always to make you laugh or cheer you up. Lancashire humour is the reason I'm friends with most of my friends, it's the one thing that I have in common with all of them. It's like knowing another language, telling a joke or being funny is a really fast way to communicate with someone to find out what they're like and whether you'll get on with them, or not. It's a way to connect. I don't think there's a better feeling than sharing a laugh with a total stranger. The humour passed on to me from my dad I've used as a survival tool for dealing with life. Humour is the ultimate form of resilience. I see this in Ethel's stories.

I think that Lancashire humour was born from tragedy and trauma. If you don't laugh, you'll cry. I imagine the Blackburn that Ethel and my family were living in and the decimation of families during and after WW1. I know that Ethel campaigned against conscription during the First World War. My dad's mum, Emily lost her dad not long after the war when she was 5 and her mum brought her up alone living hand to mouth. My dad's grandad Albert was a soldier during WW1 and he was buried alive for 3 days. My dad said Albert was a drinker and described him as a "character" because of the funny spats he got into, usually outside the pub. As my dad told me more stories about Albert it became clear that he was suffering from what is now known as PTSD. He told me that whenever he heard a loud noise, Albert would hide under the stairs and shout "tha beawn'a drop em" meaning they're going to or they're bound to drop bombs. It broke my heart imagining Albert trying to live a normal life with his family after going through such horrific experiences and then probably dealing with the guilt of surviving when his friends didn't. The same horrific fallout was being experienced and not talked about in families all over Blackburn.

Humour would've been a vital tool for coping. I think humour might've saved people's lives at that time. I don't think my dad is hilarious by accident, his humour probably comes from a place of survival to cope with the inherited trauma of his family. He is just hilarious as well. I think humour is a form of optimism that's easier to access than trying to believe or convince yourself that things will actually get better. Making light in difficult times isn't about avoiding thinking about them, I think it's a way of dealing with them. To want to make someone laugh when you're going through a bad time yourself, I see as a gift not as an indicator of an emotionally avoidant person. It's showing someone that they're not on their own, that you're in it together.

I see Ethel's stories as fables, like self-help for dealing with dark times. I wonder if she wrote the stories to help the people she lived and worked with understand themselves better because the issues weren't being discussed in the home. Maybe she wrote them to help her understand herself better? Or did she write stories to re-write the narrative of sad situations by giving the stories a happy ending. It doesn't matter how awful the situation starts out in Ethel's stories, 9 times out of 10 the ending is going to be hopeful. The underdog is going to come out on top, the limiting belief is going to be disproved and everyone is going to bed with a full belly. The overriding themes I get when I read any of Ethel's writing is a fight for fairness and freedom for everyone, but mostly for her lot.

Ethel's stories are the stories of my family, told in the same voice. Reading *Cotton Factory Shorts* stirred up memories and feelings I have felt all my life. Like in *Dick's Anconas: poultry and finance*, I've been on the receiving end of the generosity of people who don't have much but will still share it with you. Make sure you've got the tissues ready when you read that one. My mum thought that "there's always someone that needs it more than us". I didn't always agree with her. In The letter marked "Private", I've been the suspicious jealous girlfriend with an inferiority complex that I've put on to an unsuspecting innocent boyfriend. I loved this story as well because it mentions Sunnyhurst Woods, a place I walked through growing up. I see similarities to the classics in some of the stories too, Old Tom's Christmas box; the penny goose is like the Lancashire version of A Christmas Carol, if Scrooge lived in a dosshouse and drank ale for breakfast. Emily and Mark in *Courage, in two genders* reminded me of Maggie and Will in Hobson's Choice. I know Maggie and Will well because they were the characters in the first play I ever wrote. As part of my GCSE English coursework, I had to write about something that was alluded to in Hobson's Choice but wasn't expanded on. So I wrote a play about when Maggie and Will went to ask Mrs Hepworth for money; I was an expert at asking for money when I was 15.

The story that resonated the most with me is The Lucky Sixpence. It represented so many aspects of my working-class upbringing in relation to money. We used to joke about the death of imaginary rich long-lost relatives being the only way we'd ever get rich. The reality of anyone dying in our family was that certain members of the family would swoop in first and take all the stuff that was worth any money and leave all the worthless sentimental stuff for everyone else. Luckily, I loved all the worthless sentimental stuff. On the rare occasion that there was any money left to me it was usually needed to pay whatever debt I was in at the time. I couldn't use the money to honour the person who left it by buying something that would always remind me of them like a piece of jewellery or a trinket. It was spent on an instantly forgettable necessity.

My dad said his grandma Elizabeth would occasionally give him a florin and say "spend half and save half" which he'd agree to and then go and spend it all on sweets. Scarcity mindset in action, you won't get that money again so you might as well treat yourself now. After Elizabeth died they found three nylon stockings in her drawer stuffed with £100. Another feeling the story brought up for me is the sadness, guilt and shame I've felt over the years for not being able to help out my friends when they've been struggling financially because I'm usually in the same situation as them. What I love the most about the story is that no matter how poor and hungry Mary is she won't spend the 'lucky' sixpence that's been handed down to her from her aunty, who died penniless, as did the person who handed it down to her aunty.

The honour or superstition in it is beautiful and ridiculous. My mum was superstitious, I remember two of the main rules in the house were no crossing on the stairs and you couldn't pass the salt directly to my mum, you had to put it down in front of her. I can't remember why. I saluted magpies up until my thirties because of my mum. The tale of The Lucky Sixpence first appears in *Miss Nobody*. I burst into tears throughout reading *Miss Nobody*.

I didn't know why at the time, apart from the fact that I come from a long line of skrikers. I think it was because it was the first time I'd seen myself fully represented in anything I'd read. I think I cried as well because I felt proud that Ethel, possibly the first female working-class writer to be published in Britain came from my hometown. And feeling proud of Ethel allowed me, indirectly, to feel proud of myself, a feeling that if expressed in the wrong way, or at all, could be seen as too close to 'showing off' for my lot's liking. You were allowed to do well, but not so well that you'd be put in the "she thinks she's 'it'" category, just for wanting something different for yourself.

I remember the stick a couple of my friends from Blackburn got just for going to university, especially if their accent changed. A tell-tale sign of a university-goer in Blackburn was how they said "coke" or "hair" or any of the "there's". They probably changed their pronunciations to avoid having to keep repeating themselves in a noisy bar or to stop people mimicking them every time they said those words in their normal accent. Or maybe they just wanted to fit in. Whatever the reasons, wanting something different to what everyone else wants can leave you feeling like a class traitor. Like you're trying to escape your class if you attempt any sort of self-improvement. There seemed to be an unspoken rule that any kind of difference or ambition must be repressed unless it could make you a megastar and drag the family out of the mire.

In his book 'The Uses of Literacy', Richard Hoggart gave a name to the feeling I'd felt for years but hadn't been able to articulate, in a chapter called 'The Uprooted and The Anxious'. He came from a working-class family in Leeds and he was the first person in his family to go to university. He talks about the feeling that you don't fit in where you're from anymore and you don't fit in where you've ended up. It's a lonely place, he called 'class limbo'. I relate strongly to this feeling after spending 20 years working for the BBC and living a surface level middle class existence. The main middle class signifiers being the holidays I went on and the food I ate. I would tell my mum about my new culinary exploits, and she'd usually screw her face up in disgust. I can't solely blame my time at the BBC for my fancy tastes. I still laugh about the eye rolls I got off my mum and dad when, age 11, I asked my dad to bring me some brie and Earl Grey teabags back from the Kwik Save.

My dad made me go with him, probably so the cashier didn't think they were for him. I saw other working-class people working in television transition seamlessly into the middle class, all traces of their working-class roots buried only to be dug up occasionally if it meant they would come across as more 'real' or in touch with the audience. I couldn't make the total class jump because the hairs on the back of my neck would stand up every time I heard someone use the word 'chav' and the red mist would descend whenever "council estate" was used as an adjective instead of a noun; which happened a lot. It wasn't just middle-class people using those terms. Whatever class the culprits came from, I would share with them my hatred for what had just come out of their mouth.

Needless to say, I got a reputation for having a working-class chip on my shoulder. The aspiration for working class people to become more middle class to succeed is something I have always struggled with, surely, it's a two-way street. Why can't we learn from each other? Why can't I be successful just by being myself? Why do middle class people get to decide my fate? I know from Ethel's writing that she had these feelings too. I wonder if in her heart Ethel would've liked to have only written novels and become a literary darling in London but her lack of acceptance in that world meant that her writing had to appear in magazines and newspapers. Or was it Ethel's choice to make sure that her writing was accessible to working class people.

Something I wonder about is who will read this introduction, how many people from my background will read this? It's a luxury to not have to think about class, a luxury I've never had. I found it too hard because my chosen career put me as a minority in a world of privilege. I tried to ignore it over the years and just accept it and be happy that I'm there at all but I couldn't. It's at the front of my mind all the time, where's everyone else like me? Representation is everything. I've searched over the years for similarities to other working-class writers to inspire me like Andrea Dunbar and Caroline Aherne. Being introduced to Ethel Carnie Holdsworth made me feel worthy and like I'm part of a lineage of working-class women from Blackburn who will carry on writing about what they want, in the way they want to, regardless of whether the elitist gatekeepers think they belong there. No war but class war.

Jackie Thompson

As someone who came to Lancashire dialect work song in her late teenage years, I felt the same as Jackie when I first read Ethel Carnie Holdsworth's *This Slavery* intermittently in the Working Class Movement Library between volunteer tasks. The stolen hour or so devoted to a revolutionary book fit well with those who I was obsessed with - the weavers who learnt from books stuck to the loom or those who finished a lengthy shift only to then write for a few hours more. During my career I've enjoyed a position of the "enfant terrible".. that one who will risk the whole event for integrity (like when I got kicked out of the very colonial British Club in Dhaka) or will stand up on a table to prevent an over zealous folkie from starting up his tenth song when I'm sure my turn was four songs ago. Living according to your internal rules lets you forgo a certain amount of anxiety, but not much. You do begin to find the people who respect you and thus themselves in these situations, which has also meant that I've been three sheets to the wind, whiskey bottle in hand, stood on a small table belting out the Internationale in the Adelphi in Liverpool to grinning supportive onlookers. I can do this, because I live in the modern day, but I think of Ethel when I do things like those mentioned, and I wonder if she'd be cheering me on or telling me to cut it out in a gradely Oswaldtwistle accent.

Through broadside ballads I found women who were older than me, with a burning spirit which could only ever be seen by me as a catalyst for my own creative expression. Now that I'm old enough to notice that I'm not as young as I was, I am beginning to show people this burning spirit in more places so that I can pass on the torch. Like Jackie mentions, individually minded women are seen as oddballs (just ask my mother what she thinks of me) but this is our strength. I don't fancy much giving my power away, because then Ethel would have some choice words for me.

Broadside ballads were typeset by hand, letter by letter into the random, then daubed with ink for printing on a press. After the heyday of Victorian ballads (between 1820 and 1870 in my book) came periodicals and magazines as well as the usual chapbook, cocks, catchpennies and all the other assorted types of street literature. A contemporary of Ethel came to be known for his work in the Cotton Factory Times – Sam Fitton of Oldham. The Cotton Factory times was printed in 1885 by John Andrew in Ashton-under-Lyne, a hotbed of political fervour as seen through the songs of the day. When I sing Fitton's poetry in the North everyone is laughing and appreciative. When I sing it in the South it takes an audience to listen a little harder to pick up all the nuances of the work. Yes, they can understand what I'm saying, but it's the coquettish pull and push of the rhymes that lilt and flow so elegantly which I want them to delight in.

To write in the Lancashire dialect is to set alight a huge candle in a tremendous darkness. Ethel writing a single word in dialect assists me to explain and share with you her vision now. Dialect is not just one dimensional writing, it communicates everything else - the humour, the intonation, the eye movements accompanying it and how they might differ from Blackburn, to Burnley, to Accrington. It allows for the mills and machinery to come alive, for you to really understand - properly - just what it is you're reading. All that about losing your accent through education is a real fear, and Roger Miller put it best when he sang, "The people in this city call me country, Because of how I walk and talk and smile, Well, I don't mind them laughing in the city, But the country folks all say I'm citified." Its more than an accent though, its the quick pace finishing with a witty retort; its the pure poetry that flows aided by a local word here or there. Its all the way through Ethel's writing, over all too soon, because it slipped right over you and made you feel good.

It's a pleasure to write this and it's a pleasure to do it with Jackie, for Ethel. I hope you enjoy the stories and try not to feel it all at once.

Jennifer Reid

The professor's latest star: A storyette

Professor Ward's pet science was astronomy, and the greater part of his time was spent in his observatory, where he beheld the wonders of the sky through an immense telescope, which, said his colleagues, had cost a fabulous sum. The professor was in his forty-third year, and still a bachelor, to his satisfaction and the wrath of match-making mammas. He had passed through an avenue of fair women without feeling any desire to possess so much as a curl from any of them. Not that he despised the sex, but science, whom sculptors seem fond of portraying as a female, had engrossed his thoughts to the exclusion of almost all things human on this small, insignificant planet we inhabit. He was a second Eugene Arum, without the crime and before the awakening.

The awakening came, naturally, through a woman. The daughter of an old school friend invaded the sanctity of his secluded, ancestral mansion, sombre, calm, and proud, nestling amidst its rookeries. The first evening of the visit passed drearily enough for Ellen Graham. Despite her host's politeness she could see his thoughts were elsewhere. He talked in fits and starts, mixing in some mysterious fashion the theme of Hydo Park with the Milky Way.

"So you are fond of astronomy?" queried Ellen, helping herself with slim, white hands to the pickled walnuts. The professor's attention was caught by that hand. It was so delicately shaped. He remembered hearing a great scientific lecturer say that the widest difference betwixt the cultured and the ignorant lay in the hands. His gaze travelled upwards to the vivacious face, and half unconsciously he meditated as to whether her eyes were blue or grey. Of course, it was in the interests of science. Blue eyes, he believed, were weak.

"Very fond," he answered. "Some night. Miss Graham, you must come up to my observatory. Gazing upon the immensity of space makes one feel one's own insignificance. A great philosopher advises a vain man to stand beside some majestic mountain, capped with eternal snows, or look through a telescope."

"Dear!" thought the girl, "he evidently means to imply that I need the remedy."

Late that night she sat reading in her room, having ferreted out from her box of books one by Sir Robert Ball, entitled 'The Story of the Heavens'.

****

"Come in," said the professor, in response to a light tap at the door of his observatory, and to his infinite surprise his guest entered. He had forgotten all about his promise.

"I have come to look through the telescope," she said, demurely.

"Let me find you a chair," said he, making towards another room.

"Thank you," she said, "but this box will do quite as well." The professor found his guest astonishingly well-informed on comets, stars, and planets. He felt a quiet pleasure when she placed her eye to the lens of the telescope.

"You must come again," he said, as she vanished, a dainty vision in soft grey chiffon, through the door. She laughed back to him:

"Certainly; I will come to-morrow. I had no idea that astronomy was such an interesting study."

But on the morrow Ellen was seized by a picnic party, and carried off to some distant woods, and the professor felt strangely dissatisfied.

"The Great Bear does not seem so bright tonight," he said, half aloud.

****

Ellen had been the professor's guest three months. What with picnics, tennis parties, and boatings on the river with a certain bright-faced son of Britain, she had managed to get the time over, and was about to take her departure.

"So you return this day week?" said the grey-haired man of science, fixing the telescope in position, and wiping away an imaginary speck of dust.

"Yes," answered the maiden; "I shall greatly miss this observatory, and the telescope, and the stars, and — "

"And what?" said the professor.

"Various other things," she said, toying with a rose she had fastened in the belt of her dress.

"Miss Graham, you are tearing that flower," he said, calmly.

"I am dissecting it in the cause of science," she retorted with a defiant air.

"Never mind science to-night," sinking down on the chintz-covered box beside her.

"Poor science!" she murmured, with a mock pity. "Do let us talk about the starry orbs, the solar system, the Great Bear, Jupiter, Venus, and the Milky Way?"

His eye flashed.

"We will talk of a new discovery I have made," he retaliated. "I have found another star. It was the other evening, when you made that great blunder in taking Mars for Jupiter. I found it—will you not ask its name?"

She was silent.

He clasped her hand, saying timidly: "Ellen Graham, it was you."

She gave a gay laugh, saying brightly: "I knew I should win my bet."

He stared aghast, waiting for an explanation.

"I had a wager on with Philip Dewhurst. You know him—that tall young fellow who took me on the river this morning. I bet him ten to one that you would find a star outside the solar system."

The professor bowed oddly.

"Miss Graham, you have won your bet," he said, with proud self control; "but pray tell Mr. Dewhurst from me that the star I found has dropped into space again."

She slipped from the room, feeling strangely ashamed.

The professor sat up late in his observatory. The dead suns and starry wonders flashed no radiance on his soul.

"Passion is a phenomenon of Nature," he quoted aloud, "to be quenched by common sense. Professor Ward, you are a fool."

His eye fell on a glove, small, snowy, smelling of violets. He crossed over the room, lifted it with shaking fingers, looked round his lonely retreat midway 'twixt heaven and earth, then did the most foolish thing in his life.

He kissed the glove.

Cotton Factory Times, November 9, 1906

Old Jim's last looms; a storyette

The dreamy shadows of an autumn twilight were falling over the little town of Lowerwood, pleasantly situated in the Pendle Valley. Thin volumes of blue smoke curled from the house chimneys as the mill operatives returned with weary feet to their one sweet refuge—Home.

Only the poor know how dear home is. To them it is not made up of lovely frescoed walls and delicate carvings; of costly statuettes, cut by a master hand. To them it is the glint of the firelight on cheap wall paper. Each little thing that helps to make things cosy has perhaps been planned by busy brains and wrought by tired fingers. Home is not the place of abode where they recruit their strength for fresh dashes into society's pleasure grounds, but a resting place where the petty cares and anxieties of the day are forgotten; where the chain grows lighter 'neath the glance of loving eyes.

On this autumn evening the wind sighed wearily, blowing the dead leaves about in dry, ugly heaps along the lanes, and whistling through the leafless hedgerows.

In her neat little cottage old Nan Thompson sat, waiting the return of her husband, a weaver, who worked for the firm of Messrs. Bagshaw and Smith. The firelight shone on the shining steel fender, beneath which purred a sleek black cat. It smiled on the two china dogs gracing the mantelpiece, and on the old-fashioned glass picture representing a couple of rustic lovers descending a quaint stile at the end of a leafy lane.

How the wind sighed as it shook the crazy casement.

Twilight has ever been the hour for reveries, and as she sat there her mind wandered back to the 'green hills of the past.'

It had been a somewhat commonplace, uneventful life, made up as the lives of the toilers are mostly made up—of pain and sorrow and labour, with here and there a golden thread of hope and love running through it.

As a girl she had been very fond of Nature. She loved to walk abroad after the heat of the day, and watch the sun decline and drop behind the hills. In happier circumstances they would have developed her artistic instincts, but she did not know herself she was a born artist, for she had never painted a stroke, except the old window-sills in the preceding summer.

Then came her marriage with Jim Thompson in the little grey church at the end of the lane. They had one child, but she died at the age of seven, as the short-lived purple convolvulus fades with the sunny morn. They often talked of her as they sat, one on each side of their lonely hearth, whilst Jim smoked his beloved clay, and Nan's knitting needles clicked busily. They talked of all that might have been if she had lived to be the solace of their old age, forgetting that in all probability she would have been married, and the mother of half-a-dozen unruly children, with quite enough cares of her own to trouble very much about the old folks. They forgot, and perhaps it was better, for she was the only poetry of their sad prosaic lives.

She started from her dreams as the clock struck seven.

"Dear me, heaw lat he is," she murmured, half aloud.

As she spoke the door opened, and her husband, a white-haired old fellow, clad in the customary fustian, with a plaid scarf knotted around his wrinkled throat, entered the room. He hung up his cap behind the door, and sank wearily in his armchair.

"Tha're lat to-neet, lad," said his wife, and she noticed as she poured out his tea how thin and white his cheek was growing.

"Ay," he said, in a tone of reserve, and with rare womanly tact she talked of something else.

He appeared to eat with an effort. His humble meal ended he swung round his rocking chair, and gazed long and earnestly into the depths of the glowing fire. Never had she seen him so perturbed since the day they lost their one ewe lamb.

Nan hitched her chair up to his, and laid her wrinkled hand on his sleeve.

"Arta ill, Jim?" she asked, wistfully, "because if tha art ax off fer a week or two. Tha knows wey hev a bit o' brass in t' bank. Happen as mich as ever wey'll need."

He was silent, whilst the slow, hot tears of age coursed down his withered cheek. The monotonous ticking of the clock grew almost unbearable. At last he spoke.

"Aye, lass," he groaned, keeping his face in the shadow, "aw've getten sack't."

A cinder crashed on the hearth with a mournful sound.

"Never mind, mon," said his wife, cheerily, "we've ne'er bin beawt bite and sup yet. An' aw doarnd' think we ever shall. But whear hes ta bin till this time?"

"Aw've bin wandering up an' deawn t' lane, wondering heaw on earth aw should tell tha."

"Silly!" and she stroked his hand more tenderly than ever she did in the days of their courtship.

"Id wor this way, lass," continued Jim. "Mi een's noan wod they used to be, an' last week aw'd a reight mess wi' a black side. Soa, to-neet, up comes t' manager, and hands me mi noatice. He said "Tha're geddin too owd to weyve, owd mon," an' off he walked. Aw knew that afoar he towd me, but warking foak hes to wark well they con stick on their pins."

They sat and talked far on into the night, then climbed the clean but carpetless staircase.

"Good-neet, lad," said Nan, as she turned over.

"Good-neet," he answered, drowsily, and then the world was lost in sleep.

****

Nan awoke in good time. The grey chill morn was just, peeping in over the short lace curtain. She looked at Jim, but he was sleeping peacefully, so she stole quietly downstairs.

The fire soon roared merrily up the chimney, and very soon she had the tea brewed, the bread cut, and the bacon fried to that degree of crispness Jim liked so well.

"Jim," she called softly from the foot of the stairs.

There was no answer.

"Jim, Jim; breakfast is ready," she cried, louder.

7

There was no sound above, and a nameless fear gripped her heart. With unsteady limbs she climbed the stairs. The light had grown stronger, and as she stood by the bed and looked upon the placid face smiling above the tumbled quilt she knew he was dead.

She was not afraid of death: she had met him too often for that, and tenderly she closed the sightless eyes. Then she went down and called in a neighbour.

"Poor Jim," she sobbed, a little later in the day as she looked again on the face, like yet unlike, "tha'll need no looms whear tha's gone to," and then she felt as though her heart would break.

They buried him in the little old-fashioned churchyard, and the daisies grow over his grave, fitting flowers to deck the tomb of one of Nature's simplest children. Then, when the autumn winds again drifted the leaves with a dreary sound under the hedges, she, too, slumbered, and they laid her by his side.

For the poor, the feeble. and the sorrow-stricken, how sweet is that sleep where, as Christina Rossetti tells us, there is —

"Rest, rest, at the heart's core.
Till Time shall cease."

Cotton Factory Times, December 7, 1906

A bunch of white chrysanthemums: a storyette

They were really very lovely as they stood in the delicate glass in the florist's window. Graceful stalks they had, each crowned with a snowy tuft of petals, and intersected with green leaves. Jenny looked at them with wistful eyes, and wondered if they would be more than sixpence. They would look a dream on the kitchen table, but she really could not afford to pay more than sixpence for her dream. She stood at the door, a pretty picture of indecision; yes, pretty, even though the hat on the fluffy, golden head would have struck the leader of a fashionable clique as being a year or so behind the times, for Jenny Dean's beauty would have redeemed even an old poke from the commonplace.

"Well, I cannot stand here for ever," she thought, and made a sudden plunge within.

Several men were stood at the counter, presumably purchasing button-holes, but in reality flirting with the little brunette of a server.

"What for you, sir," she was saying as Jenny entered.

The words were nothing out of the ordinary, but uttered by those charming rosy lips and accompanied by a glance so bewitching they took on a new face.

"Er, aw—I'll have one of those chrysanthemums with maiden-hair behind."

"Right."

The fop squeezed her fingers as he tendered the coin, and a pained expression shot over the girl's handsome features. It was the flash of an instant, and only Jenny Dean's quick eyes detected it. She felt sorry for the girl's position. She knew enough of the world to realise that the proprietor of these London shops desired their waiting girls to be smart, attractive, coquettish. That to be quiet and uncommunicative would have lost a girl her place.

One by one the men trooped off, all except one tall, dark-haired man, who had kept in the background and spoken not a word.

"What is it for you?" said the girl, and simultaneously the two customers exclaimed: "Those chrysanthemums in the window," for the girl had looked at them both.

The gentleman blushed beneath his tan, and apologised. Jenny laughed the matter off in her lady-like way.

"You see," he ruefully added, "I have only just returned to London from the wilds of Australia, and one forgets the rules and manners of society. But take the flowers. They are yours."

Jenny fumbled in her small purse.

"What are they, please?" she inquired.

"One and six."

Her face fell.

"I did not think they were so dear," she murmured, a blush on the delicate features. "I cannot take them."

John Savage stepped forward eagerly. He would have made it a deed of gift, but he knew his ground better than that.

"They are rather dear," he said: "almost beyond my purse," with a tiny smile at the corners of his moustached-lips. "Suppose we join at the bunch?" he suggested, and his face lit up as his fair victim fell into the snare without a murmur.

She really thought he was some poor traveller returning almost destitute to his native land.

The city clock was chiming ten as the girl received her flowers.

"A Merry Christmas," said the stranger, as she turned to leave the shop.

"A Merry Christmas, sir," she responded, and then the door closed on the graceful figure.

"Have you a boy belonging this place?" inquired Savage of the girl behind the counter. "If you have, tell him to follow that lady and get her address, and I will pay you handsomely."

Lottie Berke's dark face flushed. She could do with the money badly. Her rent was due, and it was Christmas, and she had conjured up many things she would like for the winter season. Dreamt, too, of sending her brother, an ill-paid clerk with a large family, a beautiful, fat turkey; but the dream had seemed destined to remain a dream until now.

She looked into the stranger's face. He seemed an honourable man, but then she had seen so many so-called gentlemen who were really knaves. Perhaps he boded no good to the young lady, and it was Christmas Eve.

"Sir," she said, with dignity that suited her excellently, "I cannot track customers to their abodes to gratify the unaccountable fancies of gentlemen."

She laid a slight stress on the last word.

John Savage turned white, wheeled round, then answered: "I only wished to send her the rest of the chrysanthemums. You know it spoiled the bunch dividing them."

Lottie looked at him searchingly.

"Jimmy."

At the sound of her call a small boy in velveteen trousers and red coat dashed from an adjoining room where he had been roasting chestnuts.

"Yes," he said, breathlessly.

"Run to the end of the street. Find a lady with a fawn hat, with white wing, a blue costume, carrying one of our bags."

"Yes," he said again, and darted out into the night.

John Savage placed a sovereign in the girl's hand.

"Send these flowers to the address when he brings it," he said, and, with a "Merry Christmas to you," he vanished from her sight.

Lottie sat down on a basket of unpacked moss, and looked at her sovereign. Oh! the delightful vision she conjured up out of that little golden piece. She saw the steaming turkey on her brother's table, with the happy little faces crowding around, and poor Charley carving it at the head as if he had two thousand a year and a seat in the country, forgetting for a little while the office where he was starved like Canadian beef in the winter and broiled through the summer.

Then she came to herself, and her thoughts reverted to the donor.

"So he was honourable," she soliloquised. "If only all men were so," and she heaved a deep sigh.

****

"The flowers look very pretty, Jenny dear," acknowledged Mrs. Dean's gentle voice, from her couch, drawn up to the fire. It was a homely scene. The invalid mother, with her pale lady-like face peering out of the chintz cushions, and the cat asleep on the rug, and Jenny bending over her pupil's wonderful sums, for she was a teacher of mathematics.

Jenny's answer was fated never to be made. There came a loud knock at the street door, and without waiting for "Entrez," in walked the errand boy belonging the florist's shop.

"I was to leave you these," he said, and backed out without another word.

Jenny unwrapped them in amaze.

Then a faint tinge of red stole over her pale cheek.

"They are the other half," she said, and had, of course, to explain all. As they put them in the glass with the others a paper fluttered on the tapestry cloth.

It was a five-pound note.

"Oh, Jenny," sobbed Mrs. Dean, "you can have some new boots and a nice bonnet, and we will order a fresh supply of coals."

"And you shall have a bottle of the emulsion doctor ordered, and port wine. Oh; and all sorts of things," and she danced away to bring them back.

On Christmas morning, as they were enjoying the fragrant coffee and the unusual luxury of new-laid eggs, a letter was brought. It proved to be an invitation to a ball from a girl friend in the West End, who had known her at college, when Fortune smiled upon them.

"You must go, Jenny," said Mrs. Dean, positively. "You can buy some pretty silk at Ashleigh's, and I can make it up by New Year."

So Jenny went.

Her programme was soon full, and as she was whirled away a tall figure in evening suit uttered an exclamation.

"What is it, my dear Sir John?" inquired his partner, coquettishly.

"I was only wondering who that little girl in white was."

"There are so many girls in white," with a pettish tone.

"The one with the white chrysanthemums in her hair."

"Oh, that's Jenny Dean, whose father was on the Exchange—an awful gambler. Gambled them out of house and harbour. They have now nothing, not a penny, and she teaches mathematics to keep herself and her mother."

"But have they no relatives?"

"She is a haughty thing, and will support herself. Lilian Dean, her cousin, wanted her to come and sew for her, but she refused. Said she would keep her mother in a home of her own. So ungrateful of her, wasn't it?"

He smiled, but said under his breath, "Dear, brave, little girl!"

He was introduced to the girl later on, and they became very friendly. So friendly, in fact, that they both reside at one address, and on the occasion of their first stay there the hall was decked with white chrysanthemums, and she wore a long silk veil with wreath of the same, and Mrs. Dean figured thus in the society paper:

"Bride's mother wore grey satin, with old lace, and carried a bouquet of white chrysanthemums, with satin streamers. The happy couple departed for the Bay of Naples."

And so, dear reader, we will leave them, as the standard novelists say, to be happy, happy ever after. And now a Merry Christmas, and may you some day be the same.

Factory Times, December 14, 1906

Was it her duty?: a storyette

"Man that is born of a woman hath but a short time to live, and is full of sorrow. He cometh up like a flower, and is cut down, and fleeth, as it were a shadow."

Solemnly, heavily as drops of lead, the words fell on the chill November air. More heavily still they fell on the heart of Ellen Booth, as she looked shudderingly down into the dark gap which held all that remained of her mother.

"Earth to earth, ashes to ashes, dust to dust."

The lumps of clay rattled on the coffin lid; the minister concluded, and one by one the friends of the dead woman withdrew from the graveside, some wandering about looking amid the tangled grass for headstones bearing the names of kindred ones long since merged into dust. But Ellen remained looking down into the grave.

"Sitha, that's mi gronfayther's grave," said Nancy Smith, an old dame of seventy, pointing one long bony forefinger at a stone whose lettering the hand of time had filled in with greenest moss. "It's nigh on fifty year sin he deed. Eh, um! we'n o' to goa when eaur time comes, an' other foak's feet'll treyd o'er t' top o' us, just same as wey're treydin' ower theirn."

A few minutes later the cabs waiting for them at the old church gates rattled away, bearing them to the homestead that would know no more the thin but cheerful face which for thirty changeful years had been like a benediction within it. How empty the house seemed to Ellen, and the sound of the neighbours' cheery conversation as they helped themselves to the good things upon the table jarred on her ears.

"Tha're noan eytin' owt, lass," said her father, a tall, burly fellow, whose nasal organ bore a tendency to that hue known as "blush rose." Let not the innocent reader lay this down to the charge of indigestion, for it was well known that Billy Booth could drink as much liquor in a day as an ordinary individual would manage in a week.

She looked at him from her seat at the head of the table, and the sight of her dark eyes straining agonisedly out of the pallid countenance smote him with reproach.

"Aw mut ha' killed 'er," he thought, "bi t' look id gie me. Aw hevn'd bin as good as aw mut ha' bin, but id corn'd be helped neaw. Whod does id matter? We'se o' be done wi' in a toathri moar years."

"Well, aw mon be gooing," said one neighbour after another, as the shrill notes of the half-past five horn pierced the fog-laden air.

Father and daughter were left alone.

"Aw suppose tha'll be leaving ma, neaw thi mother's goan," he said at last, refilling his pipe as he spoke.

"He mut give o'er smooking for once," thought the girl, with a bursting heart, but she kept silent, looking into the depths of the glowing embers.

"Happen tha'll ged wed to thad long-faced carpenter as tha're so friendly wi'," be continued, determined to get an answer of some kind.

Even in the dusk he could see the startled blood stain the pale face from cheek to brow, and the large eyes flash as if for some impetuous reply. An inward combat was going on within her, and, raising her eyes, they chanced to rest on an old oil painting of her mother in youthful days.

"Stay, stay," the eyes of the picture seemed to implore, and she turned to the man leaning listlessly against the low, old-fashioned chest of drawers.

"Aw'll stop."

That was all, for superfluous words were not, to Ellen's liking. She was a reserved, silent creature, whom few knew and loved. Her mother had loved her as the one star of a clouded life, but all that was a page of the past now.

"We'se manige verra weel, thee an' me, Nelly," he said, complacently, now that his fears were swept away. She answered nothing, but commenced putting away the teacups.

"Aw'll just hev a bit of a walk." said Booth, his face colouring, however, beneath her glance, for she rightly guessed he was going to his accustomed haunt, the public at the end of the street. As she sat, sad and alone, there came a light knock at the door, and ere she had time to open it a young, pleasant-faced fellow walked into the little kitchen, seating himself with the ease born of familiarity on the opposite side of the fireplace. He looked compassionately at the marble-white face, and caressed with loving hand the shiny coat of Tib, who sprang purring on his knee. Ellen poked the fire into a cheerful blaze.

"Nelly," he began, timidly. "aw've allus hed a likin' for thee, un neaw as thi poor mother's goan there's nowt to stop us fro' bein' summut nearer than friends."

"Aw'm sorry tha'se spokken like this, Jim," she said, her fingers toying almost nervously with the black watch-guard dangling at her belt.

"Sorry!" with wonder and amazement in his voice. "Heaw sorry? Tha're noan beawn to stop wi' thi rascal of a fayther, arta?"

"It's mi duly, Jim."

"Duty be hanged! He's ne'er bin a father to thee; why shud tha try to be a dowter to him?" with irritation in his voice and a frown on his brow.

"Well," said Nelly, with dogged determination. "aw've med mi mind up, soa its no good tawkin', for aw'se keep mi word wodever it costs ma."

"Wilta spoil thi own life and mine for t' sake o' him?"

"It doesn't need to spoil thine, Jim," she answered, but the lines of resolve around her mouth softened somewhat, and, man-like, with all the rude eloquence of which he was master he followed up the little advantage he had gained.

For almost an hour he sat and talked to her, whilst the shadows deepened around them, and the wind rose, sighing plaintively about the ivied walls, like the voice of a lost soul which had wandered back to earth again. Ellen had conquered her momentary weakness, and all Jim's arguments were as arrows of feather shot at a wall of adamant. At last he lost patience.

"Well, good-neet. Nelly; aw'll bother thi no moare," and taking his hat from the table he passed out into the dark.

At eleven that night Billy Booth stumbled across the threshold, dead drunk.

Next week Nelly heard that Jim had become the accepted suitor of Nannie Briggs, the buxom daughter of a well-to-do grocer, and thus ended the short romance of her life.

****

Ellen was dying. A neighbour had come in to watch by the bed of the sick woman, and Booth, sobered by the doctor's latest verdict, sat alone in the kitchen below, his unshaven, bloated face buried in his hands. Selfish as ever, his only thought was what would become of him when his thrifty, housewifely daughter passed into the 'Silent Land'.

"You'll look after mi faythur a bit, Mrs. Woods?" said Ellen, her sunken eyes on the woman's kindly face. "Aw dossent leave t' cat wi' him. Tek it to yo'r heawse, for when he's hed owt to sup he's brutal." Here a fit of coughing drowned the rest of the speech.

"Ay, ay, lass; doarn'd bother thisel," wiping the moisture from her eyes with the hem of her blue check apron.

Ellen fell into an uneasy slumber, her hand supporting her grey head. The slamming of the street door aroused her, and a moment later Mrs. Woods stole into the room, a basin of something hot in her hands.

"Wod were thad? Wor id mi faythur goaing eawt?" said Ellen.

"Nay, id wor one o' Jem Yate's childer bringing this gruel for thee."

Ellen groaned. She was old before her time, being only in her thirty-seventh year, but the weary watching up late at nights, the trouble she had to make ends meet, the sorrow of meeting day by day the man who had once held out to her the chance of a happy conjugal life, but who now passed her with a cool nod, whilst inwardly wandering however he could have fancied such a plain, morose creature had broken her spirit, and made her look as if her hair had never been a shade less grey, as if youth had never painted roses on her cheeks, and all because she was denied the elixir of life — Joy.

"Naw, aw'se want nowt yet a bit," turning her face to the wall, and regarding her own shadow solemnly. "Yo can goa hoam, Mrs. Woods, for t' childer'll be wantin' their supper.

18

Aw'so be o' reight, an' thanks for o' yo'r kindness. Yo'r Matty con hev mi watch and cheon when aw'm goan," and then she fell asleep.

When Mrs. Woods returned Ellen Booth was dead, having passed away in her sleep. "Poor Ellen Booth!" many a neighbour was heard to say. And yet, why poor? The fever and pain was ended in unbroken peace.

But sometimes, on a wild night, when, the howl of the wind makes one think of the grass rustling on forgotten graves. I have pondered her story, and wondered if she had done her duty after all. Wondered if it were one's duty to repay unfaithfulness with fidelity, carelessness with care, and cruelty with love, but never have I come to a definite conclusion, but the reader may be more clever, and answer dearly to himself "Was it her duty?"

Cotton Factory Times, January 18, 1907

The Reed-hook maker's daughter

I

It was the close of a sultry August day. There was a warning of thunder in the grey, inky-black clouds, fringed with luried light, and poppies in John West's pretty garden drooped their heads languishingly as they waited for the rain that had been prayed for so earnestly in the places of worship all over the country-side. Leaning over the gate was a pretty girl of some eighteen summers, arrayed in white muslin, and with the picturesque cottage, with its gorgeous blooms and red-tiled roof as a background, she made a picture that was particularly pleasing to the eyes of an individual coming up the leafy lane, swinging his gilt-knobbed cane in well-gloved fingers.

"Stormy," he remarked, as he reached the gate, and the girl responded with an inclination of her brown, curly head, from which the print sun-bonnet hat had partially slipped. Now, whether it was the glance that accompanied the nod I cannot say, but Paul Enderby stopped, and opened conversation with the girl.

"Haven't seen you at church lately. Miss West," he began.

"No," she answered slowly. "Father's been very ill, and I could not leave him."

"But you really are in need of a change," he said, gaily. "It does not do for young folks to be cooped up too much. Particularly," with an admiring glance, "when they are young and pretty.

Lizzie blushed to the roots of her hair at the first direct compliment she had received from any gentleman. Of course, Tom Greaves, the blacksmith over the way, and a great friend of her father's, had often praised her in his rude way, but then Tom was a workman and not a gentleman. Lizzie's idea of a gentleman was one who did not work, and wore broad cloth, and looked at you as though he earned the very air you breathed. Perhaps this was owing to her simple education, or it might be due to old John West's training, for he taught his daughter that the Lord had formed two crusts to the pie of society, the lower stratum she belonged to, and the other, well, it, was made up of people such as Paul Enderby, whose father ran most of the mills round about, whilst her's supplied the firm with reed-hooks.

She felt very much honoured by the great man's remarks, and began to think it very hard to stay in and tend a sickly old man.

Perhaps he could see the impression he had made, for he was not slow to follow it up.

"Some day you must allow me to escort you to Fairy Glen," he said. "It is lovely on a summer's day. When the place is scorching elsewhere you can always find a cool corner somewhere in the glen, and the foam is flecked over the hare-bells like gems of silver."

Lizzie had an innate love of the beautiful glen, and conjured up in her mind's eye the pretty picture.

"Lizzie," called a quavering voice, and with a look of regret she went within, bidding her companion "Good-night."

The summer waned, and early autumn, with its vivid colouring, made the village lanes a bower of beauty.

II

Old John West, recovered from his illness, was coming home in the dusk. He whistled 'Annie Laurie' as he walked briskly along, but the tenderness in his voice was not loverly, but fatherly, for he conjured up a vision of his own winsome lassie, who would perhaps now be toasting the muffins for tea, or peering down the lane from beneath the pretty porch, where the roses still lingered, to be scattered by the wild breath of their fierce woer November. He had got within half a mile of his cot, when he heard hurried footsteps behind him, and, turning round, saw it was his old friend, Bob Brooks, who eked out a scanty income by keeping a few hens. Doubtless he had just come from the pen, for on his arm swung a bucket.

"Well, John, and how's this old world using you?" he said, as he overtook the reed-hookmaker.

"Well, an aw've nowt to grum'le at, as aw know on," answered his companion. "Tha knows that owd poem as were into t' skoo reading book abeawt chap as hed nowt to loise being the happiest mon on earth? Ave, but aw've eaur Lizzie to loise, soa aw moarnt say aw've nowt!"

"She is not courtin', than?" inquired Bob Brooks.

"Nay, nay, not yet. She bean't nineteen 'till Kesmas."

"Well, I've heard that she goes with — "

"Who, who?" gasped the old man. He was ghastly pale. Bob Brooks looked curiously at him.

"It's rumoured as yon lad o' Enderby's hes been walkin' her eawt," he said at last.

"Never," gasped poor West. "Unless thee an' me hes to quarrel, Bob Brooks, never dare to repeat such slander again!"

"Nay," said the other soothingly, "I only meant it kindly, West," and then they parted.

With his feeble frame quivering, he strode up the garden path, and pushed back the door with trembling hand. He did not believe it, of course not, but still he wanted to question Lizzie on the subject. The kitchen was empty, and the cups set ready on the coarse white cloth. The firelight shone on the fender, with its brass curb, and the cat rose to greet his arrival.

"Down, Tib," he said, with a push, and the sleek black thing stole back to its rest. He went to the foot of the stairs. "Lizzie, Lizzie," he called, but there was no answer.

He darted up the steps and opened her chamber door.

A scene of confusion met his eye. The drawers were left half-open, and the contents heaped in the middle of the floor, as if their owner had not had time to search for the things required, and the travelling trunk which usually stood in the corner, covered with delicate muslin, and bunched with ribbon, was gone, but the cover was flung on the spot it had occupied.

"Lizzie," he groaned again, and flung himself face down on the lavender-scented pillows that had known the pressure of her childish head — the bed on which his wife had died, and committed their one ewe lamb to his care with many words of advice.

And she was gone, the child of their love and care, on whom he had lavished the deep love of his reserved nature. She had run away. Slowly the truth lost its dreamy mists, and became more real and awful. The shadows deepened in the chamber, and, unable to bear the loneliness and dark any longer, he went downstairs.

The glint of the fire light fell on a delicate print of his tarnished jewel, and with a swift passionate movement, in which were concentrated shame, grief, and love turned to hate, he dashed it from the wall. The glass broke into a hundred pieces, but the picture lay smiling at him uninjured. He took it up, and tore it to pieces, then threw them into the fire.

"John West." he said mournfully, "you have no daughter now."

III

The wind howled round the old dwelling. Without just the same, but within, alas! what a change since last year. Twelve dreary months had ebbed away, and John West had lived alone, a solitary man, shrinking more and more from his neighbours. Ho would not even have a woman in the house to tidy up for him, but pottered about himself, to the disadvantage of his furniture and health. He got careless, and allowed the dust to gather on his household treasures, and the cinders to lie heaped up on the once snowy hearth, and would sit gazing into the embers with only one deep feeling—that of hatred against the child who could so far forgot her mothers' memory and her old father's need and honour as to run away.

After eight he always locked the door and drew the blinds to prevent the intrusion of neighbours. He had just done this now, and was puffing at his pipe for consolation, when there came a timid knock at the door.

"A neighbour," he thought, and kept silent. But the knocking continued, and at last he lost patience, and growled "Well, who is it?"

"Me." answered a female voice.

"Who's me?" he asked, his face quivering.

"Lizzie," wailed the voice. "Oh, father, let me in. I'm nearly dead with hunger and cold."

"Then go beg of those who brought you to hunger," he said, harshly. "I have no daughter, and you ceased to have a father on the day you ran away."

"But I have suffered so,." she went on, her lips at the key-hole. "Oh, dear father, do not be so cruel; let me in—let me in."

"If you don't go off I'll have the police on you," he shouted hack. There was no sound of mercy in his voice, and she could not know that the first tears he had shed since she departed were raining down his cheeks.

"Well, good-bye, then," she said, and he heard her steps die away.

He sat in the dark, feeling like one in a dream, till the clock struck ten, and he took his candle and prepared to retire. He would go to bed. Had he not always meant to go to bed and sleep as usual if ever she came back?

So he went to bed. and tried to forget how weary her voice had sounded. He heard the clock strike eleven, and then he got up and dressed, and came down into the kitchen. He had only come for a light for his pipe, but still he listened intently for any thing moving under the window, but there was the stillness of the grave. Then he sat down and wept, he forgot his pride, and only remembered that she was his little Lizzie, whom he had dandled on his knee, and that she was hungry, and homeless, and cold.

"God forgive me," he whispered, as he opened the street door and gazed into the garden. On, on, he went, forgetful that attention was being drawn to the candle. At last he found her.

She had fallen asleep under a hedgerow that has furnished her head with many a wreath of dog roses in her childhood's days.

"Lizzie," he said, holding the light close to her eyes. She started up, drawing the shawl round something in her arms, then shrunk bank as if she was afraid of a blow.

"It's me, Liz.," he said, "your father. Come home," and she burst into tears.

****

The roses are blooming round the old portal door, and just within sits an old man with long, white beard, and at his feet plays a curly-headed child with big blue eyes. The old man is dozing, but a playful tug at his long hair wakens him.

"A man coming," she lisped, and he woke to see a tall, gentlemanly figure at his side.

"Are you John West?" inquired the stranger.

"Yes."

"The father of a Lizzie West who ran away some years back?"

"Yes."

"I am Paul Enderby. I have heard she is dead, and want to recompense you for the trouble and expense that little affair caused you."

John West's eyes flashed.

He rose in his chair. "Do you think it possible to recompense a man for a daughter disgraced and heartbroken? Don't be trying to be buying a passport with your gold, for you'll ne'er manage it. And now, will you go, or, old man that I am, I shall kick you out.

He slunk away from the fiery indignation. And looking back to the lonely old figure in the porch, he almost wished he had never been born.

But the thought passed as he remembered that to-night, the Countess of B —-was giving a soiree, and that the Hon. Lady Moneyton had promised him the first waltz.

Cotton Factory Times, April 5, 1907

The letter marked "Private"

"Hal, who was that man I saw hovering about the office door this afternoon — a seedy-looking individual, short, dark, and shabbily dressed?" Mrs. Booth leaned over the arm of her husband's easy-chair, twisting her brown, toil-worn fingers in his hair, where a few silver-grey threads were beginning to show, as they will in a man fast leaving behind the prime of life, and one who has spent the greater part of his life cooped up in an editor's den.

Mr. Booth gave a perceptible start, which did not escape the notice of the clear, grey eyes regarding him.

"So many men loiter about the door, my dear," he answered. "As you know, the footpath is free." And he turned a new page of his book and began to read. His wife felt the rebuff, and, withdrawing to her work-table at the opposite side of the room, was soon engaged darning the family stockings.

As she busily plied the needle, her thoughts constantly dwelt on the man, who to her imagination, was in some way connected with her husband. She was twenty years his junior, and had come to live with her aunt in London two years ago — a plain, uncultured country girl. She had now been married eighteen months, and often, in the fulness of her heart's happiness, she chaffingly asked her clever husband what could be the magnet of attraction which drew him to her?

"Have you never cared for anyone else?" she would inquire, and it sometimes seemed to her that he avoided the points. At last she felt positive that she had obtained a clue. A clue to what? Ah! that was what she meant finding out. What had she seen? Merely a stranger near the office door; but her instinct made her conclude that there was 'something in it'. A woman's 'something', condensed, usually means another woman.

There was a perceptible restraint as they took supper together, and Alfred Booth saw in the ominous silence (for, as a rule, supper was their pleasantest meal) the first small cloud of dissension drifting across the horizon of his married life. He sat a while, seemingly deep in meditation, and twice seemed about to speak, but the thought parted away, and together they retired—the one with a deep sense of pain; the other with one burning thought—that she would find out to-morrow.

****

Early morning called Alfred Booth to his duties; and his wife, busily dressing her prattling infant, admiring with motherly pride the rosy dimpled outline of chubby arms and legs, heard the postman's rat-tat, and, giving the child into the arms of their own domestic, hurried to the door. Why did she not, as on previous occasions, send the girl to receive the letters? She scarcely knew; but, looking at the small, cramped handwriting of one of the envelopes inscribed to her husband, she heard a prophetic voice saying to her: "Within this letter lies the knowledge you thirst for!"

But she placed the letter in the rack on the sitting-room mantel-piece, and went about the day's work as usual—sweeping, dusting, nursing, cooking, polishing, and all the time the thought of the 'seedy man' and the letter marked 'private' was never out of her thoughts.

At last it became unbearable. She resolved to open the letter, read what it contained, seal it up again if all was right, and tell her husband the truth if, as she suspected, it pointed out any shameful thing in his past life. When she came to reflect, she had always noticed that Hal carried about with him a little shade of melancholy. She was his wife; of course, she had a right to his letters. Had not the minister said at the altar they were one? Had not Hal said, also, "With all my worldly goods I thee endow?" Were not letters worldly goods? She seized it, with tremulous hands.

"But," whispered conscience, "did not the minister enjoin you, the wife, to love, honour, and obey?"

"How can I honour without a light upon this thing?" she argued, and by a method she had learned at school soon

28

had the flap of the envelope unfastened. A scented missive fluttered upon the carpet. She picked it up, and unfolded, it began: 'Dearest Hal!' Her heart almost ceased beating as she read those words.

The traitor! The villain! That anyone but she should address him by that privileged title! Gulping down a sob, she read another line: 'I hope you have not forgotten that pleasant week we spent in Sunnyhurst Woods five years ago.' Another sob, strangled at birth, for she had not time to indulge her feelings until she had read all. 'Don't you remember the little rustic bridge which spanned the purling brook?' so the letter continued.

"What rubbish!" she cried, flinging it on the floor. "I will not read another line." And, womanlike, she picked it up, and continued: 'Are you married yet? I hope not. Marriage is such a halter about one's neck!'

"Married!" she ejaculated, pacing the room furiously. "I'd let her know if I had her here!" 'Come along, there's a dear follow, and spend the summer with us.' Fancy, she, that creature, who talked of woods, rustic bridges, purling brooks, and marriage being a halter, had actually dared to call her husband—Alfred Booth—a 'dear fellow!' Then came the conclusion: 'I am still working hard at my painting, and hope to make a mark yet, though I am now fast, approaching 'the first fall of the snow' period. Hoping to see you at Beech-tree Hall. —Yours sincerely—'

And then Mrs. Alfred Booth dropped on a chair laughing hysterically, for there, beneath 'Yours sincerely' was the signature of one of whom she had often heard Hal speak— Robert Pierce.

The creature, the woman, the unknown love, was no other than an old college chum.

She sealed up the letter, wiped the tear-stains from her face, poked the fire into a blaze, and put Hal's slippers within the fender, for he had told her he intended to spend the afternoon at home, and vowed in her heart to trust him for evermore. Why? Because she knew—because she had looked within the letter; because she was a woman, and she trusted, as Thomas in the Scriptures, only when she had proofs.

The seedy-looking individual was only an old curiosity dealer, whom Alfred had commissioned to bring a costly Japanese vase as a birthday offering for his young wife. This he explained to her as he put the present in her hands.

"Oh, Hal! It is beautiful." she cried; "far too good for me," and he wondered at the tear on her cheek. Man-like, he did not inquire its cause, but kissed it away.

Cotton Factory Times, September 20, 1907

A modern atonement

I

"You'll remember Colonel Jennings, Nance?"

Mrs. Williams bent her proud head lower over the work-basket on her knee, intent on disentangling a skein of silk. The exertion of doing this, for, remember, 'twas a hottest of hot days in that hottest of lands, India, brought to her usually pale face a faint flush, which had waned again ere she lifted her brown eyes to her husband's face. He looked as he stood, flicking his silver-handled riding whip, just a frank, phlegmatic, happy-go-lucky Englishman—a man whom the ordinary woman would find a most satisfactory companion in life, one who would not ask for too much affection, but take things in a cool, practical manner. But Nancy Williams was not an ordinary woman. Her grandmother had lived under the sunny skies of Seville, and something of the fiery Spanish blood coursed through the delicate, blue-veined hand sorting the silks with feverish earnestness.

"Yes, I believe I do. He stayed with the Moores, I think, a week when I did. An exquisite dancer. But what makes you ask?" And there was a note half of eagerness, half of fear, in the refined flexible voice.

"Carlton was telling me, when I dropped into his shanty this morning, that he was coming out this way shortly, and going to share his bungalow. I'm heartily glad. He'll brighten up the boys, for I never knew so entertaining a chap as Jennings. One wonders, too, where the fellow picked it all up, for he must have had a rough-and-tumble existence until old Jennings adopted him. I have wondered sometimes, too, where Jennings picked him up. We tried to pump the old beggar, but he could be as close as an oyster when he wished.

31

"Really, Harry, how very English you are," laughed Mrs. Williams. "You want to know what street a man was born in, who his parents were, what school he attended—in fact, every item from christening to your acquaintance with him, or you are eternally wondering about it. He has out-stripped you in the regiment, anyhow," and there was a thin line of scorn under-running the laughing notes.

"I never aimed high," he retorted, lazily. "Besides, it's too beastly hot in this infernal climate to have ambitions. But I believe if Jennings had been sent to do penance in the Inferno he would have aspired to be chief fire-beater. It was strange how suddenly he asked leave after you came out here, Nance. He had been telling me only few weeks previously that he hated India."

Harry Williams was no fool, and had strongly suspected that Jennings' strange mood twelve months ago was caused by his dear wife, but the fact rather flattered him than otherwise. He was perfectly sure that that insignificant dark-looking mystery could not eclipse him, and liked all his personal belongings to be admired, from his own onyx signet-ring to the beautiful partner of his luxuriant bungalow.

"Men are strange," said Mrs. Williams, without a flicker of an eye-lash.

"Well, I promised Carlton to ride over and have a game of cards this afternoon," he laughed. "That is," with sudden compunction, "if you won't to be lonely. I'm afraid I am selfish sometimes, dear, and you should remind me," crossing over to her chair, and laying his hand on her slim shoulder, gleaming through the folds of thin white silk. "I'll stay and amuse you if you like."

"You will do no such thing. What, stay away from such a party as yours promises to be, and be eternally looking at the clock whilst you think, 'the fellows will be having a rare time of it just now. Wonder what that wit Carlton is saying?' "

He smiled at her mimicry, and disappeared through the doorway of the awning.

If he could have seen his wife ten minutes later he would have thought women strange. An old Indian fortune-teller was seated in one corner, her withered hand encasing the shrinking one of the white woman's. Mrs. Williams asked some questions that evoked a quick, impetuous answer from the hag. Then, rising as if ashamed of the superstitious atmosphere, she drew away her hand, and, taking from her pocket a purse, handed the woman a rupee, and with a wave of the dainty fingers dismissed her. The woman went out with bent head, and Mrs. Williams paced the bungalow for half-an-hour, whilst the figure of her husband grew a speck on the clear horizon bounding the rolling plain, and faded from sight.

"I wonder," she said meditatively to the bowl of roses on the bamboo stand, "I wonder when he arrives."

II

The moonlight silvered the stream murmuring by the door of the Williams' bungalow. A calm, somewhat sultry evening it was, with scarce enough of breeze to wave the cluster of palms just above the house. Suddenly a sweet, musical voice floated through the still air. 'Twas a horseman, riding and whistling as he came down the hill. The tune was repeated with a precision that became almost monotonous, and it was a few bars from the 'Chorus of Faust'.

Something of stealth was in his manner, as he flung the reins over the back of his mare, and peeped into the open door, at which could be seen a bowl of red, red roses on the small table. Let us look at him by the light of the moon. Slight and dark, with a billy-cock hat shading his brow, he seemed a creature belonging to night herself.

He hesitated a moment, then whispered softly: "Nancy!"

Then, from a sofa on which she had been lying face downwards rose a graceful figure and approached the door.

"All is ready," said the man. "I was so afraid something might go wrong, but when I saw the roses my heart leapt for joy. What a clever thing to think of red roses if the coast was clear, and white ones if he was about; but come, my mare grows restive, and we have a long, long ride before us."

But she drew back, and the lace shawl, falling from her face, showed that she had been weeping.

"Come!"

The voice was persuasive, and Jennings tried to take her hand. A quiver ran over her face, and passed leaving it like stone.

"I can't!"

"Why?"

"Because it is wrong, and happiness cannot be built on wrong-doing. You would hate me, my husband would hate me, worse still—I should hate myself."

"So you will stay with that cool fool, who does not know how to appreciate you?"

"He is no fool," she retorted, "and at least," with sudden warmth, "he is a man of honour," and she vanished into the house, with a cold "good-bye".

Outside the man listened to a few minutes, then, cursing the instability of women beneath his breath, mounted his horse and rode away under the twinkling stars, that know so well how to keep a secret.

III

Harry Williams had had the malaria, and had it badly; but good nursing pulled him round, and now, weak but convalescent, he lay on the sofa, watching his wife flit round the room.

"Play something, Nance," he said. "Something rather plaintive. When a fellow has had such heaps of happiness he likes to taste of the other for a change.

Sitting down she played over the haunting melodies from 'Faust' whilst varying emotions swept her features. Suddenly her hands fell from the keys, and she bowed her face upon them. He steered in wonderment. How could he know that she could see a calm, moonlit night, and hear a horseman's whistle rings through the air? How could he know all that ever since that night she had felt one burning, mad desire to atone, to make up for the unacted but meditative wrong which might have happened but for that chance stumbling across a little pink shoe, once worn by a tiny foot now mingled with the soil of of a sequestered

English village, where she and Harry had lived the first part of their married life.

Suddenly a cry left the man's lips, full of terror. It pierced the mists around her, and she started up. Through the door had trailed in a long green snake, and its eyes of fiery hue were fixed on Williams. Nearer it crawled, making ready to leap on the invalid, whilst they watched it fascinated. Then Nancy Williams rushed before the snake and as it drew its coils up for the great leap, touched it with her dainty slippered foot. In a moment it had coiled itself around the little white form.

Then Williams rushed upon it, and with a blow on the flat, demonic head killed it, whilst his wife fell in a heap, limp and senseless on the floor.

"Nancy," he said, an hour later, "you are the silliest woman I know —and the bravest. I should have dispatched it without your aid. But I am so happy. Sometimes I have fancied you did not care for me of late, and this has shown me how wrong it was to think so."

And the devotional, religious aide of Nancy Williams' character was satisfied. She had risked her life, and what can a woman do more?

The Cotton Factory Times, April 1, 1910

Tim Reed's stocking: nature and the boy

When Tim Reed hung his stocking up on his bed rail he was blissfully unconscious of the heart-burnings it was causing downstairs, in the kitchen, where mother sat darning, and father reading, almost too intently.

Tim had noticed nothing. He was a thin, wire-strong little lad, who never saw trouble till he tumbled over it: he spent half his time dreaming, and the other half in realising his dreams. His dreams were of the type whose realisations caused angry tumult in the bosoms of old women who heard their windows being 'wound up'. His pet delight, however, was to fasten an old bulging purse on a string, select a corner well in the shadow, as the purse was well in the light, and to witness the curious human tendency to grab at money. He saw old caps and silk hats bob down with the same passion—and heard ejaculations that varied according to character, but had the common in piles of disappointment behind them. This was Tim's heaven. For had he planned paradigms he would have placed this as its highest circle of happiness.

He could not have figured in a pathetic Christmas story to save his life. His hair was too straight. He was just —boy. But if it be true that 'the good are always the merry' there should have been such a halo round that dark little head, and the face with its turned-up nose and sharp eyes, as would have lit up the drab street where he had his home.

It was surprising that two such serious-minded people as Tim's mother and father could have had such an imp. His mother had never danced, his father had never drank anything stronger than weak tea. The former was a dressmaker suffering from indigestion, the latter a house decorator, who occasionally had painter's colic. They could just manage to pay a penny per head a week to bury themselves if they happened to die unexpectedly, for Tim's mother's mother was dependent upon them in a little cottage away in the country, and would not come to live with them even for cheapness's sake, having an ambition to 'die on her own heartstone'.

Knowing nothing of this, Tim had leapt into a struggling world with a laugh in his very blood. He meant to make boots when he grew up, he said. Meanwhile he wore a great many through, and when reproached for it lay low, and said nuffin.

The strange part of Tim's composition was the secrecy with which he hid the fact of his lightness of heart from his parents. He had some kind of a quixotic chivalry which tamed down his animal spirits inside the house. Thus it happened that whatever his pranks outside had been, he entered the house with the air of a local preacher. It was not hypocrisy, either. It was an honest attempt to live up to two serious parents within the sacred precincts of the home, and the agonies that this youthful martyr had suffered from in so doing could not be told on paper.

For strange though it was, though they understood him so little, knew him so little, he thoroughly understood and appreciated his serious parents. He knew when his father was more tired than usual by the way his left shoulder was lower than the other—he knew when his mother was most bothered with a dress that refused to fit by hearing her sing, 'Oh, That I Had Wings Like a Dove,' in the weakly voice that always made him want to cry, though he would have pummelled anyone to death who had ever hinted that he was affected.

Ho understood them, but he did not let it depress him. He stood by them, was a good, quiet angel of a boy inside, ran all the errands, and try to be less heavy on his feet. Sometimes he had doubts as to how long he could play the part of the good little boy whom it would break the heart to lose, and after one of those mediations he would escape to a safe distance from the house, run to the neighbourhood where he was known as the biggest monkey let out of a cage, and would act accordingly. He had the sagacity to play where none know his parents. He hid his home address as cleverly as a forger.

And this was the lad whose nature was being so tenderly guarded by the two serious people downstairs.

There had been a painful silence in the house after Tim had walked off upstairs—a silence as after some great upheaval. Mr. Reed, being a man, spoke first, and Mrs. Reed, being a woman, seemed likely to have the last word.

"It's all right for a baby." he said. "These miraculous gifts that come from the North Pole, brought by a good-natured old man in a dressing-gown, but what will Tim think of us when he finds out? Tim is a serious child. You can see it in his eyes. It will be a shock to him. He'll never believe in us again."

"You'll take all the romance out of Tim's life," half-sobbed Mrs. Reed. "Think how he looked that morning when he woke, and saw them all—and he did so want a cobbler's set, and oh, it won't be the same when he knows."

"He's got to know some time," said Mr. Reed. "Now, Mary, this is a serious matter. Don't let us make light of it."

"Light of it," expostulated his spouse. "Richard, do you think a light-minded woman would read Hall Caine? Look on the book-shelf, and let that answer for me. Besides, Richard, when Tim was born, remember all the books we read on children."

I sometimes think," said Richard Reid, "that no one will understand the child till some child writes a book about itself, and it would sooner play, I'm afraid. No, I take that back. Tim might do it. Tim is not a common child. He takes life seriously. That is why I have always thought we should have to be very careful with Tim, and Tim's upbringing. There have been times, Mary, when I've felt a desire to take that lad by the shoulders, shake him, and have a romp— and it would have made me younger. But he has always looked at me so seriously, that it kind of scared me. When I was a child I got no childhood —I could have had one with had one with Tim, but since he is as he is —" He sighed, got his pipe, and lit it.

For three solid hours by the clock they went over every point of the case, always with the consideration of Tim's temperament before them, as a vision—and in the end they decided that Imagination was a greater loss than Truth, and that for another year at least, for their part, Tim should not be robbed of the ice-palace with the coloured windows wherein abode a famous traveller, the Patron Saint of the Child Universale.

****

It was in the silver dawn that a ghostly little figure stole into their room.

"Just the things I wanted," said Tim, jubilantly, gratefully.

"Good boys always get their reward," said mother.

"I'll make a pair of shoes to-day," said Tim, passing over this praise hurriedly, and crept back to bed.

"Tim's so modest," said Mrs. Reed, sleepily.

"I think that boy will grow up to be a genius," said Mr. Reed. "He's so quiet. Any other lad would have jumped round the room. He's an enormous reserve, Mary. Perhaps he'll be an actor."

"I can imagine him playing Hamlet," said Mrs. Reed, and without the knowledge of how this opinion would have been shared by the people on the outskirts of the town, she fell asleep.

Tim did not say much about the source of his cobbler's set. They took it as a sign of faith so deep that it was reverent. He looked very disappointed when they told him he must put his toys away and attend a tea party with them, but obeyed meekly, was put into a clean collar, and they set out. They went on the car. Tim looked through the car window a little uneasily. His mother had to ask him to sit still twice, to her great surprise. She did not know that Tim was aching to get away from the sight of those familiar windows he rattled, whereat he expected to see familiar faces.

"Are we going a long way?" he asked once, hopefully.

"No; we get out here,." said his mother.

"This is not our chapel," said Tim, unwillingly.

"I believe Tim will be a Conservative," said his father, thoughtfully.

Tim looked about him very carefully when he got inside the large schoolroom. His heart began to get lighter as he observed no face that he knew, and by the time they were seated at the long table with the celery glasses and jam, and brown and white bread, and cakes with sugar, his fear had become a shadow.

"Mine wouldn't sit still like that," said a stout woman, with a sigh of admiration towards Tim.

"Tim's a fine lad." said his mother.

"Of course, they say when they're too old-fashioned an' quiet they never live to grow up," said the stout woman. "There's no danger o' mine deein'."

"It's a question of temperament," said Richard Reed, who loved four-syllabled words.

"Aye, their tempers are a bit different," said the stout woman, "but I allus thinks there's summat wrong wi' 'em when they sit still so long. She had suddenly discovered reason to be glad that her children were rough. She was also looking at Tim in a questioning sort of way, as if puzzled. When tea was all for all the children had drifted together to play, and the elder folk sat round, before the concert began. Suddenly a little woman came to the stout woman, they conversed, and Mrs. Reed noted their looking towards Tim.

"They've taken a fancy to Tim," she said.

Mr. Reid nodded.

"I'm glad we bought that ticket from poor Sarah," she said. "These children may learn better manners from Tim, an' they can't spoil his, Richard, for Tim can't be spoilt."

A puffy-looking man now joined the stout woman and the little woman, and again Tim was scanned closely. The man evidently asked to whom the prodigy belonged, for soon he made a bee-line towards the adoring parents.

"That your lad?" he asked solemnly.

"It is," they answered in chorus.

Again the man scanned Tim from head to foot. Then he looked back at the serious yet shining countenances, stamped with patience, calm, and the meekness that comes from lack of energy.

"Ay," he said. "I shouldn't ha' thought it."

There was something strange to his tone. Mr. and Mrs. Reed woke to the fact that the tone was not altogether suited to the words.

"Yes, he's ours," said Mrs. Reed.

"Well—" The man paused as if conscious that what had been on his tongue had been too strong for a Sunday school. "Well," he said, "if I catch him playin' with that lad o' mine again I'll break his back, so warn him. We can't do no good with him after this imp o' yo'rn has paid one of his visits, for he comes down here like a lion let loose. I didn't know if it were him at first. Sunday clothes makes the difference. But it's him all right. It'll hardly be safe for you to let him come down here again, for there's several folks waitin' to take him in hand, seein' he's been brought up as if he lived in a wood. That's all I've to say, except this—if that lad does die i' bed it'll be a marvel to me."

"Tim!" said Mrs. Reed, faintly. "It can't be Tim!"

Mr. Reed was watching the puffy man walk in Tim's direction. He saw the sudden look of consternation on Tim's face, of recognition, and of guilt. He was shaken to the depths of his being, this father of a genius in embryo, and his face worked queerly. Mrs. Reed also was moved. She also, following his eyes, had seen.

They had lost a unique possession.

Mr. Reed suddenly let out a yell of laughter.

Mrs. Reed shrank back at the sound, her eyes swimming with tears, then laughed hysterically, then naturally.

"He'll live to grow up!" said Tim's father.

And some time later they learnt that it was Tim who had destroyed the faith of half the children down that way—the faith in the ice-palace, where dwells the Patron Saint of the Child.

They had taken Tim too seriously!

Cotton Factory Times, December 24, 1915

Ducks: the tragic story of a village Romeo and Juliet

Margit leaned across the tea-table, laying her rough hand on her old man's. The smell of the factory was scarce blown from him, for he had only had to walk the length of two short streets from the mill. To Jerry Cross this firelit hour with Margit over his pint pot of tea, with the cat perched upon his shoulder, rubbing her soft coat against his neck, and begging for bits, was ever one of the brightest spots in the grey day of toil. Margit had generally had her tea when he arrived, but ate another crumb or two and had another cup of tea to keep him company, whilst she retailed to him the doings of the street. She could neither read nor write, but her mind was anything but a blank, and she had the keenness of a Sherlock Holmes in ferreting out secrets, motives, and piecing one and one to make two.

Jerry, unlike his usual way, was staring into the interior of his pint pot, as if reading terrible things there.

"Ged thi tay, lad," urged his spouse. "Tha' morn't go off thi meyt, whatever happens."

"Ay," he answered, almost groaningly. "Tha's fair knocked mi appetite into th' middle o' th' next week!" There was a pause, then he added, with a forlorn gleam of hope in his eyes, "Arta sure it wor eawr George?"

"Jerry," said Margit, very firmly, "my e'en aren't as sharp as they wor when fost I clapped seet o' thee, but aw could tell mi own lad in th' pitch dark, an' ther wor a glimmer o' moon. It wor eawr George an' that 're Susanna Mason, for aw soed her red heyd agen his coyt. A nice thing! Him talkin' soft into th' ear o' a lass as her father and thee wor enemies — an' a' through him as we had to close eawr shop, for if theirs hadn't been stuck at that corner we could ha' had a nice comfortable living, and tha' wouldn't have to be moilin at the mill like tha are now. An' look heaw they put them cakes in at a hawfpenny cheaper nor hours — an' them great cards they had in th' winder, sayin, 'Our eggs is new laid,' as if eawr's weren't! And folks comin' in our shop to feel how hard the cheese wor, and then goin' into theirs an' findin' theirs a bit softer, an' not comin' back! An' aw'll allus believe to my deein' dat 'at it wor them set them analysin' chaps on to look into th' lard, an' it worn't your fault it weren't pure, for we hadn't bred the pigs, an' so they browt ruination on us, an' a' eawr bit o' brass as we had worked for us all hard for went — just through them Masons! And look how Susannah used to lick her tongue out at George, an' now the're canoodlin' agen heawse-ends, an' lickin' one another's chops like a pair o' young cauves! But it's got to stop. It hasn't to be. Aw've said it, an' aw'll howd to it. George is two an' twenty, but aw'd knock him down as soon as look at him yet. An' the little maddlin' is doin' nowt but laugh at him, aw'll lay, or else it's getting a wimp that George's gronfather has promised to leave him a' his brass. An' if George wed it he'd bring it here, an' aw'd sooner dee in the workheawse, Jerry, nor ha' that snigh-nosed, flour-faced, gigglin' hussy stuck here an' callin' thee father and me mother!" Margit's voice shook like a fiddle-string. It was now Jerry's turn to comfort. But he had barely begun when there was the sound of cheerful whistling, the beat of steady feet coming up the garden path, and the door was whirled open, and in a moment George was standing in the little kitchen.

"Get my tay out sharp, mother," he said in his genial way. "Aw've gotten to get off like a flash o' greased leetnin'."

"Ay," said Margit, slowly. "Well, aw'll ha' to put a sup more watter in th' kettle; but it'll soon boil up."

"Oh!" ejaculated George. Then he said cheerfully: "Never mind th' tay, mother. Aw'll do neawt to-neet. They say it's bad for th' nerves."

"Ay," said Margit. "It just depends heaw strong it is — like luv."

George gave her a quick glance, but she was imperturbably setting him his plate and spoon in the way that always reminded Jerry of an old hen feeding its chick.

In spite of all his mother could do to delay him George was ready almost as soon as a flash of greased lightning is ready to flash. He scuttled off with a hurried "Good neet, if you're i' bed when I come back," which was impudence itself. But a sudden thought turned him back in horror two yards from the door. He was in the cottage again.

"Is my neck washed right, mother?" he asked breathlessly, like a great schoolboy.

Margit looked at it critically, lifting up the lighted lamp to the task, and sending the light this way and that.

"Well," she said slowly. "Tha' must ha' given thisel' time to wash what soap off tha put on. Tha'd looked weel if hoo took a notion to look deawn inside thi collar."

George looked at his mother, reddened, appeared to decide to take her in jest, then darted across to the looking-glass. Turn his head as he would he could see no trace of dirty soap-patches.

"You're having me, mother," he laughed, and was off. The door closed after him. Margit looked at Jerry, now smoking his pipe in the ingle-nook.

"Aw'me noan hevin' her," she retorted, in answer to George's last remark. "Jerry, arta boawn to sit theer smookin' a' th' nect whilst eawr George is rushin' to his own destruction wi' yon red-headed maddlin'?"

"What con aw do?" asked Geordie helplessly, hopelessly.

"Do? Out but sit theer like an owd owl!" snapped Margit. "If aw hevn't brains enough to put mi spoke i' th' wheel aw'll stick mi yed in the broth-pon the next time aw hev id on th' fire."

She went out, and returned in half an hour.

"Well?" queried Jerry.

"They were stuck a' amongst th' muck i' Lovers'-loyn," she said disgustedly. "Tellin' one another what they liked i' th' eatin' line, an' what they didn't. I expect they'd getten fast for summat to talk abeaut." Then a smile overspread her face.

"Well?" asked Jerry, pulling out his pipe.

Margit leaned forwards.

"She mortally hates savoury ducks," she said, "An' them as eats 'em. Ay, Jerry lad, whatever tha sees me do or hears me say durin' this next week don't be gloppot or think I've gone crazy. It said it wouldn't wed into a family whear they ate such things as penny ducks!"

Then she got her knitting and Jerry went on smoking. They were sitting up when the lad came in.

"Ay, wo'd shoon, George!" said Margit.

"Ay," he admitted. "it's a bit mucky reaund bi' th' slaughter-heauses." Margit shot a glance at Jerry to ask him if he'd ever heard owt like that, for the slaughter houses were in exactly the opposite direction to the Lovers'-lane.

"When arta bokun to bring her to her tay, lad?" she asked, quietly looking over her glasses.

"Bring whom?" asked George.

"That lass o' thine," said his mother.

"Con aw?" he asked eagerly.

"Ay, lad," said Margit, with assumed warmness. "Bring her next Sunday."

"Hoo's a bit bashful," said George. "Con hoo bring her mate wi' her?"

"Ay, th' moar an' the merrier," said Margit. "And aw'll hev such a spread for her hoo'll think we mista'en her for the queen."

"Aw know you'll make a good tay, mother," said George. Soon after he went to bed — as pleased and flustered as if someone had left him a fortune.

Margit went out that very night to Bill O' Sandy.

He was just about to shut up.

"Hev yo' ony savoury ducks?" she asked him.

"One or two left fro' Saturday," he said.

"We'se be mekin' fresh to-morn."

"A'll tek them tha has," said Margit.

"It's aw reet if they're etten reight off," said Bill. "But I wouldn't advise yo' to keep 'em knockin' abeaut."

"Awl shouldn't think o' it," said Margit.

"Thear!" she said to Jerry when she got them laid on the table. "Aw reckon they'll be a' reight bi Sunda'!"

"But," said Jerry. He was sniffling a bit as it was, and stuck his pipe in sharply.

"They'll ha' veils on if aw put 'em in that damp hoyl under th' stairs," she said, gloatingly.

Jerry shook his head, like another MacBeth.

"Jerry Moss, that hesn't the courage o' a cockroach," said his wife.

All that week she appeared to be making a great stir to have the house spick and span. George seemed as if he could not believe himself.

"Aw didn't know yo' knew, mother," he remarked once. "But if yo' knew her as weel as me yo'd know yo' were justified in layin' th' best befoor her." Then he said something about her shyness.

"Ay, luv is blind," said Margit to Jerry. "Shy! That maddlin' shy! It's moar cheek nor a brass monkey, an' aw'll see at my lad isn't ta'en in wi' it. Aw've me e'en open if his are shut."

The Sunday dawned clear and sunny. Margit was in the kitchen, cutting bread and butter. Jerry was in his old nook, a little perturbed, but solacing himself with his pipe. George was in and out, "like a dog at a fair," looking at the clock every minute, Finally he put on his hat and said he would go and fetch them.

"Margit," said Jerry, warmingly, "they're here."

The next moment the front door opened, and George was heard telling the girls where to put their things.

"Aw'm pleased to meet yo' both," said Margit, in answer to George's mumbled introduction.

"Aw'm pleased to meet yo'," said Susannah Mason.

Her hair was redder than ever, but she did look a little toned down from the pig-tailed child who had licked out her tongue at George. George hovered near her. He saw that she had the best chair, and let the pale, dark-haired girl with the mole on her cheek perch herself on an ordinary chair. He stood and turned the music pages while Susannah sang 'Excelsior' in her rather nice voice, and the sight made his mother boil with rage. The other girl looked on with a demure pleasure. Eventually she left the parlour as if she felt herself somewhat in the way, and came into the kitchen.

Yo're i' black, aw see," said Margit.

"We've just buried my mother," said the girl.

"You never miss 'em till they're gone," said Margit. "Though what they do is little thowt on while they're here!" She sniffed. Jerry looked uncomfortable.

"Awm sure you're well thowt on," she said. Her voice was remarkably muffled. She was a little pale round her lips, a little teary round the lashes. She looked a trifle uncomfortable, too, and stared at the tea-caddy on the table as if she did not know where to look.

"Ay, we're all right," said Margit, "but we soon get our noses put eaut out of joint when a nice lass comes along." Jerry moved restlessly.

"Could aw not help you to mek th' tea?" said the girl. She had flushed from brow to chin. Margit found her the tea-cups and ordered her about. She seemed grateful to have something to do. After this Margit told her to camp Jerry, seeing that nobody else wanted her — this last remark being accompanied by a significant glance towards the parlour door. Again the girl blushed crimson — nervously sensitive to the slight on her friend. Then she sat and talked to Jerry. She knew an enormous lot about dogs and horses, and Jerry and she got on capitally. Margit came into the kitchen from the scullery to find Jerry allowing the girl to light his pipe —a rare mark of favour.

"Tea's ready," Margit called to the two in the parlour. Susannah and George came out.

"Here, thou can sit aside o' her," said Margit, as George was about to take the chair next the dark, pale lass. She jerked her thumb in Susannah's direction.

"Nay, aw'll do varra weel here," he said, with a look at the other girl which puzzled Margit. However, she was thinking of the ducks, and had not time to bother. She noticed that the lass he spoke to seemed a nervous bit o' cattle — and knocked her fork to the floor, as if she were not used to being looked at. Susannah, however, was taking a full survey of the kitchen, pictures, old furniture, some of it tied up with string, etc. Margit saw her and laughed to herself.

"Bide a bit," she was thinking. "Bide a bit, miss, and thou'll feel wor nor that."

The tea-table was literally groaning with luxuries such as it was not used to — pink blancmange, port wine, jelly, cream biscuits, a trifle with silver pellets on its snowy whipped cream froth. Susannah approved of the spread.

She looked across at Jerry and spoke to him patronisingly — of the weather. Jerry had a haunted expression on his face, and his replies were somewhat vague and wandering, and Susannah clearly thought him a fool.

"Have we no meyt, mother?" said George.

Then he turned to the pale girl.

"Tha mun ha' a bit o' meyt," he said, in a somewhat friendly manner. "It'll do thee good."

"Ay, lass," said Jerry, "that looks like tha'd do wi' a beef-steak a foot thick wi' some fried onions at top o' it." The girl blushed and smiled. It was like a revelation, that smile; so slow and sweet, like late sunshine on a chill landscape.

"Yigh, we've some ducks," said Margit, slowly.

"Ducks!" said George, thinking that his mother had indeed made a spread fit for a queen.

"Ay," said Margit, slowly. She went into the kitchen.

"Jerry!" she called in a few seconds. "Bring a dish for these ducks."

Jerry did as he was bid.

Margit, choking with laughter, lifted the pan-lid from the vessel on the gas-jet. The odour escaped, and Jerry began to cough. He plucked her sleeve, and mee-mawed that she could not possibly put that hash on the table; but with lips grim and set, Margit emptied the contents upon the dish.

"Carry it in, Jerry!" she commanded.

What a scene followed! Through the stench and steam that came from the ducks Margit, like a veritable Fate, ignored the askance look of George, the disgust of Susannah, the despair of Jerry, and asked everybody politely if they would like a little duck as if the course she offered were what it might have been from her grandiose tone.

"No, thank you!" came Susannah's icy answer.

"Will thou ha' some, Jerry?" asked Margit, as if much surprised.

"Nay, aw'll no bother, lass," said her spouse, humbly. "Aw gets a bit sick o' 'em." He was that flustered that he had played into Margit hands by speaking as if stale ducks were their common fare. Margit's eyes twinkled. She was beginning to thoroughly relish the position she had created. George looked upset, but not so much so as she had fancied he would look. Evidently thought love would be stronger than a prejudice on the part of his girl not to wed into a family that partook of savoury ducks. But George had always been a model for filial respect.

But Susannah's face was a study.

The indignation painted upon it would have served to turn a dairy of cream sour. She looked as if she could scarcely manage to sit upon her chair in the face of that awful incense from the dish that was set directly in front of her.

"Will thou ha' some, George?" asked his mother.

An exclamation that would have begun a speech to say she knew he could not bide them was stopped by Margit.

"Well, tha happen does get sick o' 'em," she said, pleasantly. "I hope you like ducks," turning to Susannah, "an' you're sure to be fain eaur George likes 'em — for they're cheap and an' soon made ready, and you'll find it a savin'." Susannah stared icily at Margit, at Jerry, at George, and at her friend.

It was clear that if ever she had seriously thought of entering the Moss family she had irrevocably changed that opinion. George was going red and white, and looked at his mother anxiously, as if afraid that she was going crazy, or that she would insult Susannah's bosom friend by asking her to partake of the duck.

Even as he looked the blow fell.

"Now, thou'll ha' a bit," said Margit, coaxingly.

The pale face flushed. Something like a smile, but so faint that it was almost imperceptible, crossed it.

"Ay," she said heroically. "Aw'll tak' the least bit!" Margit gasped. That anyone would eat that stuff had never entered her head. The lass must be hungry; she looked half clemmed. With the spoon in the dish Margit paused, fearful lest she poisoned this girl, but in a dreadful quandary. The lass had said she would take some. There was nothing for it but to give it to her.

Meanwhile Jerry was fumbling away with Susannah's plate. But Suzanne ate little of anything. And in truth the stench from that dish appeared to have penetrated everything upon the table. There were awkward silences and jerky beginnings of conversations, and Susannah was evidently in an awful temper. Susannah's little friend, however, struggled with the duck, though she left a portion of even the tiny serving Margit had given her. After tea the young folk adjourned to the parlour. Susannah's friend came out after a short time, and helped Margit to wash up. Listening intently, Margit caught scraps of conversation that sounded like a quarrel.

"Thanks very much," said the pale, dark girl; "we've had a nice time," ten minutes later. "If ever yo' feel like comin' to see my father and me, aw'll be pleased to see you; an' seein' you're so fond of ducks we'll be sure to ha' some for you, just as gammy as these were."

There was a sly humour in her grey eye that told she scented something funny in the whole proceedings. Susannah was putting her stylish hat on, and jabbing the pins into it as if she jabbed it through George's heart. She would barely say good-night, and seemed in a dreadful hurry to be gone.

"That's done it," said Margit to Jerry, where the door closed after them. "There'll be no Masons wed into this family, an' when eaur George's a little older he'll thank me for what aw've saved him fro'."

****

"Whatever hev yo' bin tryin' on, mother?" asked George.

He had come back, only having been out half an hour.

Evidently he was very much annoyed, and Susannah had broken with him.

"Aw med up mi mind tha' shouldn't ha' yon scornful hussy," said Margit.

"Scornful hussy!" said George, angrily. "Who are yo' talkin' abeaut?" Jerry interposed here, trying to pour oil on the troubled waters. And after some five minutes of jumbled, angry talk George burst into irresistible laughter, making his mother stare through her tears.

"When yo' try to mek bother between courters," he said, "be sure you've gotten howd o' which is which. Susannah Mason goes wi' my pal, an' we're very much alike in the dusk, an' often ta'en for one another. Ann Thomas is my lass, an' her father has just ordered me out of the house for good, for he's as nooky as he's loaded wi' brass. They live up at that farm on th' hill yon, an' ha' ducks every day if they like, an' Ann has had a college eddication, but can talk same as gradely folk, an' never took to th' larnin'. An' if she were poorer nor a crow aw'd ha' had her. But yo' doarn't know what her father is. Carries a gun, too. An' a chap o' his word. An' when he see poor Ann's face as she had to stagger up to bed, an' the doctor coom an' said she had been half poisoned wi' some mak' o' bad meyt, he just ordered me out. Aw durn't tak' much notice o' Ann, her bein' so shy. Aw expect that's heaw yo' get wrong."

He ceased.

Margit sat down, and began to rock herself behind her blue apron. Peace was made eventually. She went next day to see Ann, and sitting in her old bonnet with the jimped edge ten years behind the fashion, and telling the tale over to Ann's father in her rude way, she somehow or other got to his heart, for he burst into a gust of laughter that shook the rafters, asked her to stop to a dish of tea, and said he was sure that a son of her's was fit even for his daughter Ann.

Cotton Factory Times, February 18, 1916

The open door

Jimmy o' Jeff's laid down his paper with a loud sigh of satisfaction.

"The'ar!" he remarked to Mary, his wife. "I knew it wod come, lass; though I mun say 'at I never thowt it would be i' eaur time. 'Tis th' breakin'-up o' sassiety—an' everybody's as good as everybody else. I can believe it, for it's in th' paper, an' this chap 'at tells abeaut it is larnt-up. Neaw, we'se happen ged to see a bit o' life—though we've hed it dree an' steady a' these years. I allus thowt I'd like to see an' mix wi' th' upper ten afore I crept down under the daisies. I dare-say it's in th' blood, like; for mi' grandmother wor a servant i' a real hall, an' thowt a lot o' th' upper classes, ay, reight to her deein' day. Hoo said 'at they med mistakes sometimes, like onnybody else; but their hearts were in th' reight places — if nobbut yo' could ged at 'em. An' neaw we've gotten a chance."

Mary was intent on ironing Sarah Ann's mill-apron. She had just got the tip of the flat iron on the plucker that led straight across the middle of the string, to lay it smooth at one sweep. She had heard the drone of Jimmy's voice much as she heard the ticking of the grandfather's clock in the corner.

"If tha'll tell me wod tha'rt chawin' abeaut," she said, in her dull, slow tones, "happen I'll know wod it's a' abeaut."

Just then she heard the ceasing of the scales that Sary was working on in the parlour. She clipped her lips together.

"Fifty pounds for that piano," she said, "An' I've to go on at it like a ninny-hammer, or it wod flit in an' out o' that parlour just as it liked. I nobbut wish I'd a chance to larn th' piano when I were young!"

Hurriedly setting the flat-iron on the top of an upturned saucer, she swooped into the parlour. There, surrounded by the wooden-looking photo engravings of dead relatives, by cheerful mottoes of religious note, and with a picture of the Maiden's Prayer looking down on her, a small girl in a mill apron that nearly touched her feet was sleepily regarding the dotted notes on the music-book. Her sleeves were rolled up, showing a pair of arms reminiscent of a plucked cock chicken. She had large, soft brown eyes that blinked at the candle-light, mouse-coloured hair hanging in two plaits down her back, and a pale complexion. In a few years she might develop into something of a beauty. Just now she was all arms, legs, and very sleepy and dull.

She saw her mother standing in the doorway, and touched the keys again.

"Come, Sary," said her mother, "tha wants to ged on wi' that playin'. Fifteen bob a quarter it costs thi' father an' me. There's lots wod ha' bin fain o' th' chance. Tha wants to read th' life o' them musickers i' th' weekly paper—an' heaw they had to play i' cowd garrets. I reckon there's lots o' them Pader-whiskies would ha' bin fain o' a fire like that an' their parents drummin' at 'em to keep 'em at it. Soa, go on, for it's thi' only chance whilst tha'rt young—an' mind tha doesn't drop ony fat off they candles when tha puts 'em eaut."

"I'm that sleepy, mam," said Sary Ann. "I'll practise to-morn o' th' neet."

"Tha only wants to come an' hev a marlock wi' thi father," said Mary. "Neaw, go on—an' do thi heaur, that's a good lass." She closed the door.

When sho got back into the kitchen she found that the flat-iron had slipped from the saucer, and was scorching a hole in the ironing-cloth.

"Couldn't tha smell owt?" she asked Jimmy, disgustedly.

Jimmy looked up from the depths of the fire, in which he seemed to be reading pleasant pictures.

The light of dreams was in his eyes.

"Could I—what?" he asked hazily. Then he saw Mary staring at the brown mark. "Eh, I didn't know there wor owt burnin'," he said, apologetically.

Mary's grey eyes filled with tears.

What wi' tryin' to ged musick out o' eaur Sary Ann, an' sense eaut o' thee," she said wearily, "I'm fairly at th' end o' mi tether. An' then, look at th' sort o' washin' days we've hed latteley, an' flour gone up agen, an' the Zeffelins flutterin' abeaut like gret buzzards I' th' dead time o' th' neet! It's enough to drive onnybody gawmless. An' I doarn't know whad I've done to ha' such things put on me."

A kindly light shone in his eyes.

"Tha'rt stall'd, lass," he said, understandingly. "Come an' sit thee deawn in th' nook, an' stick thi' feet inside th' fender, an' let's ha' a crack. We've ne'er hed time for one for soa lung 'at we're soart o' forgeddin'. Or tha con sit on mi knee, if tha likes—"

Mary laughed.

"Sit on the top-bar," she said. "I'd as lief. But I think I will sit deawn, so how be it. An' wod isn't done mun goa undone." She began to put the cloth, iron, and saucer away.

"Ay, sit thi deawn," said Jimmy, "there's no virtue I' goin' on till tha drops deawn like an owd hoss, 'at hos to be ta'en to th' knackers'. Tha mun start an' think weel o' thisel', Mary lass, for tha'rt as good as onnybody—bar noan—for it says soe in this paper. We're a' equals, neaw, same as folk were when there were nobbut Adam and Eve; an' he had to cleyn th' hen-muck up for hissel, an' hoo hed to do her own weshin'."

Mary looked at him.

Then she burst out into laughter.

"What art ta laffin' at?" asked Jimmy.

"Nowt," she said, and then, after a little bustling about and shutting of drawers, and tidying here and there, she ordered Jimmy to fetch in a big cob o' coal, and they'd have a camp together over the fire.

"Neaw," said Mary, "wod were ta sayin', owd lad?"

Jimmy found up his paper, cleared his throat and read the paragraph that had struck him in the article of the intellectual.

"There's no more class distinctions," he explained, "they've goan. He says so. They're washed away i' streams o' red blood, an' wey're a' brothers an' sisters neauw. 'Tis a middlin' big price to pay, I know, but — "

"Onions is threepence this week," said Mary.

"Ay, ay," said Jimmy, hurriedly, "but listen. Tha does't seem to realise wod a gret barrier has bin shifted fro' th' path o' the workers, Mary. There's no moar class distinctions! Why, thad makes thee a soart o' relation to th' mayor, an' further nor thad, id brings us into line wi' them o' the bluest blood — "

"I wish oawr Sary had a bit moar blood," said Mary. "Her lips are a bit too wishy for my likin'."

"I wish tha'd ged away fro' th' personal." sighed Jimmy. "Doesn't tha see, lass, wad it means to ha' this owd barrier shifted eaut o' oawr gate?"

"Noa, I doarn'd," said Mary, densely.

"Well," explained jimmy, "we can go onnywhere. I expect they'll be doin' away wi' fost an' third class carriages, soon. Of coorse, we mun give 'em a bit o' time. But—well, id just means 'at thee an' me is Somebody, whereas we were nobody afore. Eawr Sary'll reap the benefit, I'm thinkin'— for there'll be nowt to stop her weddin' a dook, seein' as a' th' human race is a soart o' relations."

Mary's eyes glistened.

If there was one point on which she was gullible it was on Sary. She sat back and listened to Jimmy's dreaming of the Millenium for half an hour. Then he went out to walk along the darkened streets and smoked his pipe, and musing on the great challenges that had swept him near to the great. Meanwhile, Mary pleated Sary's hair for morning, giving her hints to hold her head up, and think so small beer o' herself, for the rising generation was going to be honoured.

Sary listened.

"They'll happen pike thee eaut to be th' Rose Queen this year," went on her mother. "Though, heaw I'm to ged thee a satin frock wi' silk roases warked on I dearn'd know. An' I think tha'd better stop ca'in' us mam and dad, an' ca' us ma and pa, for I dearn'd mind goin' hawf way to meet 'em, seein' at they've made med the fost move."

"Good neet, ma," said Sary, then she commenced to giggle and nearly fell in the middle of the stairs.

"Shut up, tha lumber-foot," said Mary "or tha'll waken thad kid next doar. Id oppens it's e'en if a flea crawls up th' wa' —."

Just then Jimmy came back.

He sat down in his old corner.

Intense excitement was written on his face.

"Sitha," he cried, holding out a bit of white card. "I foun' this on bi' th' Parade."

Mary put on her glasses and read.

"It's for us reight enough," she said, her voice snaking. But—it doesn't say nowt abeaut Sary."

"Uh—they'd tak her for granted," said Jimmy. "But isn't it a bit of a' right, Mary?"

Mary read the words on the card out aloud.

"Mr. and Mrs. Simms present their compliments to Mr. and Mrs. Jeff, and desire their presence at an 'At Home'. First Wednesday. R.S.V.P."

"Tha'll be geddin' off thi wark," said Mary. "An—but never mind. It'll be worth it. An' it'll be a start I' life for eawr Sary. She might go cout mates wi' that Simms lass—an' larn a two or thri bits o' ways off her as'll be handy later on."

They sat up till past their usual hour, making plans for the great event. Consequently, Jimmy fell asleep after the knocker-up had been and gone, and Sary an' he had both to run off without a sup o' tea through the cold, dark streets, that were like a vault.

"Ne'er mind, Sary." said her father, "things'll be awtered in a bit. They've said as thee an' me an' thi mother were brothers an' sisters o' theirs, an' after they've acknowledged us they can't go on sarvin us like this. We mun gie 'em a bit o' time to change things. An' it'll soon be Wednesday, sohowbeit."

****

Jimmy sat dressed in his best, by the parlour window. watching his pals go off to the factory. Mary was finishing herself and Sary upstairs. The quarter buzzer had gone. It had seemed queer to sit and hear all those feet going on without him. It was ten years since he had had half a day out of the regular holiday, and then he had had lumbago so bad that he hadn't been able to appreciate the luxury.

It was a clear, windy day. with swift white clouds sailing

over a sky of rare blue. He heard the sparrows chirping in a bush in the garden, in the lulls between the clogs coming out from the little houses, and the slamming of the doors.

"Art ready, lass?" he called at the foot of the stairs, when all was silent.

"Ay, we're noan late," said Mary. "But we'll go a good hawf heawr befoar th' time, an' then they can't think a' th' warking-classes is dilatory —"

So Jimmy sat and smoked his pipe, and watched the curling wreaths until the clock should strike two. Mary sat in the room with him. Sary played 'O Touch Those Chords'.

"It's thad nice I can hardly think it's true." said Jimmy. "Well, I reckon we'se ha' to be off."

They went out and along the sunny streets. It was a fair distance to that house in West Parade, the house at which they had looked wistfully o' nights, as Mary passed puffing with carrying her week's shopping, done at half a score of shops, to get the cheap line at each.

At last they reached it.

Mary had taken Sary up a bye-street to wipe the dust from her shoes with a handkerchief, once, and Jimmy had rearranged his tie several times. They surveyed each other now, and saw themselves reflected as perfect in each loved face.

"Thee fost," said Mary.

"Ladies before gents," said Jimmy.

Sary was looking at the terra cotta eagle in the centre of the lawn; at the crocuses and snowdrops that looked like bits of snow; at the shining knocker in brass, and the steps that had taken a domestic three hours to clean, starting in the dim shivering dawn.

With a pleased smile of wonder on her little pale face she advanced as one entering fairyland.

Jimmy nudged his old rib.

"Sary's noan freetened," he said. "Neaw —what is there to bother abeaut? They've axed us, an' wey've come. An', after all, tha'rt as good as Mrs. Simms."

"An' I wouldn't swap thee for ten Mr. Simms," said Mary. "Come on. Look whear Sary is."

It was Sary's pale finger that pressed the bell. A man-servant opened the door, revealing a glimpse of scarlet-covered stairs. Mary set the man down as some relation of Mr. Simms, and so did Jimmy. Sary was taken up with the number of buttons he wore.

Without a word Jimmy o' Jeff's handed the card to the servant. He looked at it, then at the group before him. A curious smile flickered over his face, but was gone on the instant.

"This way, Mr. and Mrs. Jeff," he said, and flung open the door of a room, bidding them make themselves at ease, as Mr. and Mrs. Simms would be down presently. It was a grand room. Jimmy, who had a fondness for pictures, walked round, looking at them, whilst Mary was pondering on the probable thickness of the carpet. Sary picked up a look of fairy tales from a chair, and began to read, regarding the wonderful illustrations with awe.

There was a sound outside on the polished floor of the hall, then a servant girl entered. She started on seeing the room occupied.

"How have you got in here?" she asked.

"We've come by invitation," said Jimmy.

Mary's eyes had glinted with antagonism at those words, spoken in that tone.

"Happen we've blown in," she said. "Or maybe we've bin dropped off a flittin'. What's it to do wi' thee, onnyroad? An'—"

"She hasn't sin it in th' paper," Jimmy reminded his wife. He looked at the girl in the white cap and apron. His blue eyes regarded her with a kindly look.

"We're a sort o' relation to Mr. and Mrs. Simms," he said.

"Oh," said Susan, and smiled. "I'm very sorry."

"Don't mention it," said Mary, genially enough.

"Your cousin," said the maid to Jimmy.

"Brother," said Jimmy, sticking to the literal wording in the article he had read.

Susan looked at Jimmy.

There was a puzzled look on her face.

The man sat there, with a comfortable assurance; a look that said he knew he was welcome. Mrs. Simms had been poor in her early youth. But she had not heard that he had a brother.

"Your brother will be down shortly," said Susan.

The couple nodded.

Susan intended to go upstairs and acquaint Mr. and Mrs. Simms with the unexpected arrival of their relatives, but the back-door bell rang at this moment, and she was faced with the milkman, and, being an arrant flirt in her spare moments, the thing went quite out of her head, and when she returned to the kitchen she found that she had barely time to get the tea things ready.

Meanwhile Mary, Jimmy and Sary were getting a little tired of their long wait. But just as their patience was on the point of giving out they heard the rustle of silk down the stairs, and then Mrs. Simms stood in the doorway. They knew her from her photograph, well-known to the local press. She was a stout, middle-aged female, with what now appeared to be a stony stare.

"Show her th' card," whispered Mary to her husband.

Jimmy sat and regarded Mrs. Simms with a frank geniality.

"We've come," he said, in his slow accent. "Th' postman mun ha' dropped th' hinvitation card i' the street. 'T'were just luck as I should find it."

"I-I'm afraid I don't understand," said Mrs. Simms.

Jimmy nudged his wife.

"Jeff—eawr name is," she said.

Mrs. Simms looked, almost gasped, then recovered somewhat, and smiled faintly.

"Oh—I'm pleased to meet you," she said, and held out her hand to Jimmy, who rose to his feet, and gripped it till she almost screamed. Mary took hold of it next, but not so rigorously. Sary advanced shyly, and smiled.

"Excuse me a moment, won't you?" murmured Mrs. Simms, and left the room. In the huge, dark red-plushed room next to this one she vacated she found Mr. Simms.

"They've come," she said, in despairing tones. "Oh, Will! They're worse than we expected. What shall we do with them? And the others will be all be here within a quarter of an hour."

"I've been asking them to come, on and off, for twenty years," said Mr. Simms slowly. "'So we must grin and bide it, and set them the best we have, and those that don't like it, Matilda—well, they can lump it."

The door bell rang.

Mrs. Simms wrung her hands.

It was Dr. Mackie's wife, newcomers to the town. She put her in with the Jeffs, and left her to her fate, as the bell tinkled again.

"Bring tea in, Susan," she said in tones of depression.

Tea was brought.

Mary spread her handkerchief upon her knee, and told Sary not to drop any liquid on the carpet, and Jimmy sat beaming at the assembled crowd. He was in the daze of a golden dream. The millennium had come. They were amongst the great. To-morrow! But why care for the morrow. But at length it was time to go, for everybody else had gone, and Mrs. Simms was still waiting.

"Thanks for a gradely nice afternoon," said Jimmy. "I believe i' th' brotherhood o' man fro' this heawr. An' if ever you come down Lilac-street drop in for a cup o' tay; but don't come o' washin' days, for they're rather cheerless."

"Lilac-street," gasped Mrs. Simms.

The truth was beginning to dawn on her.

Those creatures, the spoilers of her afternoon, and maybe the cause of her being ostracised by the Muggins and the Juggins, were not the couple to whom William had owed his life, and the start he got in it.

"What did you say about the postman?" she asked.

Her tones had utterly changed.

She looked at Mary, Jimmy, and the girl as if they were applicants for soup or forgers of a passport.

"I said 'twere lucky I foun' it whear be dropped it," said Jimmy.

"What is your Christian name?" asked Mrs. Simms.

"I was christened James, but allus get Jimmy," said Mr. Jeff. Mary had risen, and stood close by him. Sary was looking scared.

"You have been mistaken for old friends of Mr. Simms," said Mrs. Simms icily. "My good people—James." She raised her voice slightly and the man in buttons came, with that same curious smile, flickering for a moment, to be replaced by a wooden and inhuman look.

"Show these people out." said Mrs. Simms.

Mary gripped Jimmy's arm.

He stood flabbergasted, and she heard him mutter something about the brotherhood of man.

"Four bob for a weaver," said Mary. "Jimmy, tha'rt a foo'."

Then she said with a laugh: "Show these people out."

Jimmy said nothing.

He walked out with bent head, seeing his dream vanish.

"Come on, Sary," said Mary, "an' howd thi heyd up. Tha's nowt to hing it for. If onnybody gaet i' eawr heawse bi mistake I reckon we'd know heaw to treat 'em, an' yon Simms' woman didn't.

Cotton Factory Times, March 31, 1916

The advent of the dog: a converted wife

Sally o' George's, buxom, and with some of the dust and ashes of the Friday's 'cleaning-up' upon her (particularly visible on her great arms), surveyed the wisp of a man who stood before her, phlegmatically chewing tobacco, but with something of furtive anxiety in his brown eyes.

"I tell thee, Joe, 'at if tha brings that pup here, I'll walk out as it walks in. Isn't there enough o' wark tha's provided me wi', tha great noodle — six childer, an' th' youngest twins, an' me weshin' three shilling's worth a week to buy thee a new suit — and now that wants to bring a dog. A dog! Tha'll set me slavin' after a dog as can't bring nowt in, neither neaw nor onny time. I can't walk reawnd th' heawse for childer under mi feet, and neaw tha'll bring a dog. Tha owt to be ashamed o' thisel', but tha'rt like o' the rest o' thi sex — an' to think tha used to ax me to ha' thi muffler on o' cowd neets for when we stood campin'!"

Sally's voice, never that of a turtle dove, had increased in volume until it could be heard without ear-strain by any one three doors higher up.

There were two things Joe usually did under these circumstances of irritation. He either went very quiet and threatened to stop her jaw, in a still, firm voice; or crumpled up with a "Neaw, lass" and gave in. Both these moods meant exactly the same, by result. Sally waited for their appearance now. Then she stood flabbergasted, for Joe did neither. He merely moved towards the open door, which showed a night sky full of stars, saying only, "I'm fotchin' it, Sarah."

"Tha'rt what?" asked Sarah, and followed him to the door as if to prevent him by physical force. But Joe was gone. Sally went round the lamp-lit kitchen, clearing the children's small, faded, much-mended clothes away. Murder-thoughts were in her mind, and had they been effective Joe would have fallen stone-dead at the end of the first block of houses. As it was, perturbed, but whistling 'Tipperary', he plodded on through the dark streets, almost colliding at the corner of Oak-road with a thick-set man, whose voice in a round oath Joe greeted with a "Hello! Just goin' to fetch that pup. Come and ha' a look at it. Tha said tha would, Grimes."

They went on together until they reached a house standing by itself — a dark house in a field — with the sound of mumbling and crumbling, yelping and snarling, issuing from its black body. It was the house of Draper, the dog-man.

A man-faced woman, in clothes that might easily have been taken for the casts-off of Noah's wife, let them in.

"They've come for th' pup, Jim," she said, in that tired voice, to the huge fellow sitting in a great chair by the fire, a pot of frothing ale on the hob beside him. There was a suggestion of tears in her voice.

"We've come to look at it," corrected Joe, standing by the dresser, and appealing to the man he had brought with him as a judge.

"Ay, to look at it," backed Fred Grimes.

Joe and the dog-man's wife were now listening to a crooning they came out from the scullery. So Joe missed seeing the meaning smile that passed between Grimes and the dog-man. It was not the first time that Grimes had acted as impartial judge of Draper's dogs, helping him to palm off some inferior animal upon an amateur.

"Fetch it, Becka!" commanded the dog-man.

The pale-faced woman with the big grey eyes trailed off, as bidden, and re-issued with a dog in her arms.

"Be still, Major!" she said.

A red, rough tongue licked her wan, thin cheek, and then Joe saw that her eyes were swimming with tears.

"Don't like to part wi' it, eh, Missus," he said, a little awkwardly, and feeling at the same time that 'Missus' was an ugly and suitable title for that childishly slight figure, that soft, pale face with the big eyes.

The dog-man looked callously at his wife's emotion.

"Called after a bloomin' chap who used to take her out walkin'," he cheered. "That's why. She's spoilin' th' darned hanimal. That's why I'll let it go so cheap. Now, Grimes, straight and square, isn't that the best little Airedale tha's seen this many a day? No bluff! Isn't it? Look at it! Dark, squinty eyes, good colour, an' bone — biggest boned dog o' th' litter that, bar noan. Square jaw, long head, and lively. Put it down, Becka, and watch it go!"

Becka set the dog down.

It certainly acted as if it contained within its small body a whole galvanic battery.

"That dog," said Grimes, very weightily, "will take the shine out o' the champions o' th' countryside. I can sort o' feel it, and when I get a feelin' like that — well, it's never missed yet."

Upon which Joe picked up the dog, felt at it, got the red, wet tongue of it roughening against his cheek, and felt a thrill — a thrill ages old, the thrill that a dog brings to the heart of a man who has somehow or other in toss and tumble of life still kept a child-heart. All Joe's ancestors had had dogs. It was the wakening of a passion hundreds of years old, had he known it — but he couldn't, for his family tree was held in the twilight mists of obscurity.

His grandmother had been a washerwoman, that was all he knew; his grandfather would, in mathematical terminology, have been written have been written as X, but in reality he had been a country laird, with an over-weaning fondness for wine, women, and — noble and redeeming feature — dogs! So all this struggle now in the heart that pulsed within that leaden-tinted, narrow-chested weaver man, with his dominant wife and his bunch o' babies, and he knew not whence it came, only that he felt within him, fierce as a flame, the desire to take all that tumbling bit o' dog, though it meant leaving the 'divi.', which Sally had drawn that very day, behind.

"Home much for it?" he asked wistfully, and in three minutes the bargain was concluded. Minus fifteen shillings, half as much as he could earn in a week at his "hell-hole", he travelled home with the pup. Grimes said he would be along soon, but Joe got tired of waiting for him. How he would have stared could he have seen that judge of dog-flesh laughing at his innocence, in company with Draper, over a jug of ale fetched by the draggled wife.

"I shouldn't wonder," she hazarded timidly once, as if defending something precious, "if Major turned out fine, and deceived you both."

"I know dogs," said Draper. "That was goin' to be a sailor tomorrow, Becka, if he hadn't come for it. But, didn't th' ginger liven that dog up? In the morning'! — "

He drowned a loud laugh in his pint pot.

In the morning! Joe came down to go to work two hours before his usual getting up time. During the long and weary night he had had feverish dreams of something yowling in the corner of a cube sugar box placed before the downstairs fire, with his best overcoat over it for additional warmth. He had likewise floated ideas of voices from neighbours on each side, and of Sally saying in his ear-hole, that even the twins, cutting their eye-teeth, had not come near that racket!

Now, weary-eyed, he lifted the black leaded fire-horses from the box lid, and took out the dog Grimes had vowed would be the despair of every fancier in the countryside. Then he stood aghast. Then, with frantic hope he dashed to the window and drew up the blind, thinking the dim light of the kitchen responsible for this sad metamorphosis. The "regular, romping, storming puppy," who would walk home with first prizes round his neck, and a knowing blink in his canine eye, was a dull-eyed, apathetic, drooping and whining brindle from whence all the spirits seemed to have flown. He had been sold! He knew it. Sall —! He shuddered at her coming remarks. She would place the dolly-tub in the yard, and bid him drown it!

He shuddered again at a recollection of a mangy cat he had drowned for old mother Gibbs. He had carried the pup home in his pocket. It was licking his hand now. He — couldn't do it. He had been sold. That pup was a rickety thing, and maybe had no pedigree. Well, had he any pedigree? He put it back in the box, and went into the scullery for a saucer of milk, moving as cautiously as possible. But when he got back into the kitchen and there was Sally, sleepy-eyed, a twin in one arm, her tousled hair and tremendous size giving her an Amazonish look.

"Taking milk out o' thi child's mouth — for *that!*" she said, fiercely. "*That* win prizes. Look at it."

She flashed such scorn down into the corner of the box where the pup cuddled that Joe wondered if it did not wither up under the lightning. Again that vision of the tub shot fear through his heart. The thing was no good. But it was his. He must bluff Sally, somehow.

"The dog's not in good condition," he said. "Draper has neglected it. That's why I got it cheap."

"Cheap!" ejaculated Sally. "Why, man, thou paid twice for it what tha got me for." And she dashed off into the scullery.

And thus commenced a struggle for and against the pup, the struggle of a determined woman and of a no less determined man. Whilst through it all, with its life trembling in the balance, the conscienceless pup ate up a pair of the twins' shoes, help to drink a part of the twins milk — and Joe went on half his usual tobacco rations to provide the rickety, crooked-legged specimen with a half-pound of raw beef in the week. He likewise squandered a penny weekly on 'Our Dogs', as if, said Sally, he was a millionaire! Her bangings about made as little impression as her tears. That pup had come to stay.

Joe spent his evenings in the fields, walking the bandy-legged animal about. He had begun to have a curious faith, unsupported by scientific reasoning, but nonetheless fervent, in the pup. The fact that it had the world against it only strengthened this fanaticism, or perhaps it was the hypnotism of his own eternal suggestions to Sally that the pup would set them all up in the world by turning out a champion stud dog, who would sire the best dogs in the countryside. Any how, the more he looked at it (though even small boys sniggered as they watched it walk) the more he was convinced that Grimes, Draper, Sally, and the world in general, would be deceived in that dog, for that it certainly had all the points Draper had mentioned.

Meanwhile, it provided a Keystone comedy for the street, to see the pup bandaged up, and with Joe tumbling over things as he went backwards way, ticing it to do anything but crawl, with bits of meat, though it looked, in scriptural language, as if it intended to 'go upon its belly all the days of its life'.

The climax came when Sally, dressed in her best, and with the twins in their pink frocks, and little Billy and Sue in their best, also stood before Joe, who sat, after a hard day's toil, in a rapt vision, watching the pup attempt to frisk as if it had some spasm of youth. He had been utterly unconscious of anything but that strip of carpet and the dog for the past half-hour. He believed the pup was on the mend.

"Going out?" he enquired, dreamily, as he saw the little procession before him. And then he was startled wide awake by remembering that it was years since Sally thus dressed herself on a week-night, and particularly after a big day's washing and ironing.

"Ay," she said, "I'm going hoam to mi mother's till tha sends me word tha's drowned that thing. And if tha't long i' sendin' I'll bring thee up for persistent cruelty and desertin' thi wife an' family, and squanderin' thy fortunes on a dog. I'll leave thi Ted and Minnie just to find thi summat to do —to play wi' like, seein' tha might ha' enuff wi' *that*."

And she was gone, leaving Joe in a stupor.

He went to the back door and looked after her when he roused himself. But she had reached the end of the row, it was broad daylight, and a chap who had once been sweet on Sally was smoking and watching the scene from his yard door, and Joe remembered that they had been married twelve years, and it didn't beseem a man's dignity to run after a woman, under all those circumstances. And when he got back into the house he believed Sally would come back next morning. If she didn't, he decided that she wasn't worth having back. To leave a man with two childer on his hands, and besides, who would feed the pup in the middle of the morning and afternoon?

When he had kissed Sally under the hawthorn in Lovers' -lane he had little thought it would come to this. Parted— by a pup!

He had to call in Ted and Minnie, and put them to bed. Meanwhile, through all his agonies and the chaos of his next week's housekeeping, the pup went on its puppyish way. Joe paid two shillings a week for a woman to take Ted and Minnie in from school time to the mill turning out, and — to feed the pup. And all the time he imagined that it was mending. Visions of dog shows, with himself triumphant, and Sally repentant, began to float before his eyes again. The struggle between himself and Sally began to resolve itself into what appeared to him a fight for his manhood. Sally had always crowed it over him because she was bigger, he thought.

But he got very miserable.

The house felt cold and damp, being without fire in the daytime, and empty, too, without Sally, the twins, and the other two.

But he was determined not to show the white feather.

He sent Sally fifteen shillings and a brief note to say that he and the family, pup included, were well, and as yet undefeated. That night, however, he was awakened by violent pains.

In three hours he was in the grip of pneumonia, and the woman next door advocated sending for Sally. In four more hours she had arrived with her little train. And, jaded as she looked by her sojourn in a house where children were always in the way, and where she had only stayed as long rather than give in (to the pup), she set to fight for Joe's life. In the long watches of the night his incoherent ramblings about the pup brought tears to her eyes. She brought the dog up and put it on the bed once or twice, but he did not know it was there.

"Eawr Tom says if yo're moithert wi' that dog, he'll buy it off you," said the woman next door once.

"Not for nowt," said Sally, sharply.

"Nay, he thowt yo'd enuff to do with a' them childer," began the woman.

"Nowt at th' soart," said Sally.

The next day the pup disappeared.

"You've not sin' Joe's dog?" asked Sally, over the yard wall.

"Noa," she answered.

Joe's dog! That was how the Sally looked on the nuisance, now. The dog that Joe had thought so much of. He might die. It was Joe's dog.

So, whilst Joe's sister looked after him she nipped on her shawl and ran up and down the street after street, calling "Rag! Rag!" for that was the name of Joe's dog. As she flew past the end of the fourth street she saw two men. One had an Airedale pup in his arms. They were laughing.

"Thought I'd get it," said one. "Now, how much for it?"

It was Grimes and Draper.

"Nay, I'll sell it to thee," said Draper. "'Twer mine. Yon' mon is at death's door. An' his wife had six kids; she'll noan bother. That dog, mon, is worth—why, the fool knew more about dogs nor us. I thought 't would croak in a week!"

"Hand that dog over to me," said Sally, turning from the shop window into which she had pretended to be staring, her face half-hidden by the shawl. "Before yo' take dogs that are lost you want to be sure they're lost. I'm Joe's wife. That's our dog."

She walked off with it cuddled under her shawl.

When she reached home Joe's sister was crying in the kitchen.

"Why, Polly," choked Sally, standing with the pup in her arms, her red cheek paled, "is he dead?"

"Noa," sobbed Polly. "He's taken a turn for the better. I am that fain."

Sally was on the stairs, pup in arms still.

"Theer!" she said, regardless of the doctor, seein' that Joe was now conscious, "that's thy pup, owd lad, an' it's that much of a bargain 'at them as sold it thee have thought it worthwhile to habduct it. So I reckon thou wer' reet!"

She set the pup down, and it commenced to walk up towards Joe's face, beginning to lick his ear. Sally snatched it away when the licking turned to biting.

"It's—it's a devil!" laughed Joe, in a ghost-like voice.

"An' neaw tha' wants to get ready for th' show," said Sally. And from that moment Joe made rapid progress.

****

A small newspaper paragraph to the effect that Joe had had an offer of two hundred pounds for Champion Crompton Orang Major, a young nine months old pup, competing in a local show, appeared six months later, and it is good to be able to tell how the derelict dog became a famous sire, unconsciously retrieving thereby the fortunes of those who had entertained an angel unawares. His pedigree, in gilt frame, hangs over Sally's mantelpiece, and she has got from him an affection that only takes place next to that which she holds for the twins, though how much it is based in economic materialism the sentimental need not inquire, as to do that might be to bring in sordid and political elements. But even then, the date of her conversion in Major's favour might still stand as upon the very day, when she was summoned to attend a husband at death's door—a fool of a man who loved a dog and knew not why.

Cotton Factory Times, June 23, 1916

The Lucky Sixpence

"Mary, lass, thou mun keep this sixpence, whatever happens to thee. It were thy Aunt Belle's, and she kept it through hard times and easy. Maybe it'll bring thee luck."

Those words, spoken by her dying mother, were ringing again in the ears of Matty Brierley as she stood looking in at the window of a grocer's shop, where crusty brown loaves, all arow, made her hunger feel twice as keen. For she was very, very hungry. No one would have thought it, because she held herself well, and her shawl was well-mended, her clogs ashine and black. But by a series of accidents, scarcely possible—even in fiction, but true in life—she had come to be without money. In another fortnight all would be well again. She knew that. But fourteen days seemed so many eternities to look ahead, and know that in all the world she had nothing but that lucky, crooked sixpence, which, judging from the destinies of those who had possessed it before, had brought nothing about poverty and struggle.

A faint smile, too sad to be sarcastic, stole over Mary's face, as she thought of poor Aunt Belle's luck, and of her own mother's. She knew, too, that Aunt Belle had become possessed of that crooked sixpence by having it given to her by the clammy, dying hand of the little shirt-maker to whom she had been a friend. It had been all the little shirt-maker had to leave, all Aunt Belle had to leave, all Mary's mother had to leave, yet they had all had faith in it.

Those crusty loaves!

Mary shut her eyes tight, and moved away from the window, and as she did so collided with the young man.

"Can't you look where you're going?" she said sharply, out of the misery of the hunger and uncertainty ahead of her. It was utterly unreasonable but human. The young fellow looked at the face under the sailor hat. There was nothing shrewish about it. It was a plain face, except that the eyes were so startlingly blue, the hair so very brown.

"I'm very sorry," he said.

But Mary had turned the corner of the street without looking at him.

She turned into one of a little row of houses in a gray, gritty street. It was full of clothes a-drying, clothes that looked, Mary's mother would have said, "as if they'd been boiled in th' porrich-pan, and dried up the chimney". There was a crushing engine at the lower end of the street, throb, throb, throb, like the beat of a tired heart. Mary went up to her bleak bedroom, and the throbs of it seem to go right through her.

"Miss Brierley, three letters have come for you," said the voice of Mrs. Smith from the foot of the stairs.

Mary went downstairs, and into the untidy kitchen.

The little place always seemed full of work and children, children of all ages and sizes. As she looked into the eyes of the draggled woman she lodged with, Mary was glad that she had paid her lodgings a month in advance. She was not taking bread from the mouths of those puny children at least.

"There they are," said Mrs. Smith. "I hope they've good news." Mary smiled. The Smiths had no idea that she had nothing but the crooked sixpence. She had thought they might ask her to eat with them, and she knew the children went short as it was.

She opened the letters standing by the end of the dresser, littered with bundles of clothes come to wash.

One was to say that as four stamps were missing from her insurance card she could not claim money until they were put on. The other was from a friend from whom she had half been thinking to borrow a pound.

The other was a cold note informing her that her Uncle John James, cranky, crotchety Uncle John James, had died in the workhouse, and was she prepared to go anything towards the coffin, as it might make folk talk if he was laid in a pauper's grave.

Somehow or other she managed to get upstairs with these letters.

She read the one from little Annice Bond again.

"Dear Mary", it than, "I should not have liked to ask you if I hadn't known you as I do, but could you lend us a pound for a month only? Baby has been ill, Tod has a place (he's been out of work ever since you left Little Hareton), but it won't be until three weeks are gone that he can go—and, oh, Mary, my heart breaks to see little Tom's thin arms, and his big eyes frighten me so, and I must get him nourishment somehow. His people thinks it serves us right. We were very young, I know. We'd both die before appeal to them. We've pawned everything, and, ugh, what a dreadful thing it seems to pawn! I feel sometimes like jumping in the canal that goes just by the door—only, of course, there's the dead dogs and cats, etc. I'm laughing, Mary, but, oh! I can't see forward after all. You just can't see what it's like not to be able to see forward. I know I shall get help from you, and I've no more pride in crying out to you than I would have—to God!

—Ever your loving *Annice.*

Tears had blurred the last lines to Mary's sight. Dear little Annice. She would have given her her blood, had that been any help. She laid the letter down, saying over to herself a line from some verses she once read, saying them with a big cry in her heart that loved to give: 'Poor, amongst the poor'. Yes, so it was. She was helpless among the helpless.

And it had never entered Annice's head that Mary was not doing well, for she had left Little Hareton to mend herself at the great, new, prosperous town, where she had fallen ill through sucking infection through the shuttle when she had gone as 'sick weaver' to the great new mill with its thousand rattling looms. Then the little purse, containing money enough to see her through her sickness even without insurance, had been picked from her pocket on the way to the chemists. When she had got sufficiently well to return to work she had found that the looms promised to her for 'regular' had been given to someone else, and her turn postponed. Now she did not dare to get work elsewhere less she lose her turn at the other mill, and everything was in such a mess and a muddle, even to the not be able to draw the pound or two she had in the post office at Little Hareton, owing to the postponement of withdrawals due to the auditing, that she knew not which way to turn. In a week she might get the money, meanwhile—

Then she read over again the letter from cousin Lucy regarding Uncle John James. They had sent him to the workhouse, then, the old man, because he had been sick so long, and his sickness had been the horrible one of cancer. She remembered him, cantankerous, peculiar, as he had been in his old age, and then she recalled him, younger, under happier circumstances, bringing apples for them in his bulging pockets. It hurt her that Lucy should speak as if she were collecting for a stranger. He was a Brierley. A pauper's grave. Mary shuddered. Yet what could she do?

She laid the two letters down on the little bamboo table, and between them she placed the crooked sixpence. She shook her head sadly at the sight. She sat there until it was almost dusk. She heard the feet of the other factory toilers going past the door.

They were going home to tea.

She held her hand pressed to the place where the horrible gnawing was going on, and on, and on. Then she looked at her sixpence. What luck had it brought anyone who had had it? Why not go and buy bread, hand it over the counter to one who would only see in it a common sixpence? That was it. It was not the faith that it would bring luck—it was its associations that made it hard to part with it. Aunt Belle, the little shirt-maker, her mother—always keeping it, through direst poverty. Why, it had gone through the Cotton Panic days, and yet had not been spent. It seemed sacrilege to spend it on bread that would be eaten soon. But when she had sat there another hour she remembered that if she did not write to Annice, her little friend would think her cry had fallen on empty air. Then there was Lucy's letter to answer. Two stamps, and one of those crusty loaves. Then the keepsake would be gone.

Five minutes later she was on her way to the post office. She passed inside the lighted room, where people were getting postal orders to send off.

"Two penny stamps, please," she said. Poor little Annice. The refusal was better than silence. A pang was in her heart at parting with the coin. It felt like selling the dead.

The stamps were handed to her.

She put her hand in her pocket.

The purse was gone. She felt again. No, it was gone, really gone; gone with the only coin she had in the world.

"I—I'm very sorry—must have dropped my purse," said the little weaver to the postal clerk. Gone! Bread, stamps, and the luck of the unlucky Brierleys. She got out into the streets, and began to search.

"Could you lend me a match, please? I've lost something."

The young man addressed started, looking for the second time into this girl's face. He saw that she did not recognise him. The tone of voice was different from that sharp one in which she had first spoken. It had a dull agony.

"Certainly. Perhaps I could help," he said, and lent her a box of matches.

"Don't trouble," she said, but already he was peering about on the ground.

"A purse," she said in answer to his inquiry.

"Had it much in?" he asked.

She had just dropped a match, and its light flickered over her countenance.

"All I had in the world," she said between laughing and crying. Then she puckered her brow in annoyance that she had told so much to a stranger. Soon after she went on her way, but he saw her at intervals for a time by the flicker of a match. Then he turned and followed on, though keeping well in the background, so that she should not see him still searching.

At the corner of a street he found a purse, opened it, discovered the sixpence—the crooked sixpence—and the folded sheets of two letters. The envelope with the address of the one they had been sent to had evidently been destroyed as too bulky to go in the purse. All she had in the world! A lucky sixpence!

His search to find her proved unavailing.

She had disappeared.

Then he went on his way to work. An hour later he was startled by hearing a voice from another room. It was clear and firm—two qualities he had remembered in that other voice. It must be! Three times in a day. He looked through the open doorway. Yes. There was the shiny black sailor's hat, the grey shawl—the girl he had met twice before. She was standing looking into the pimply face of the moneylender.

"Could you lend me five pounds on a bank book containing twelve?" she said, in a business way.

"Your own bank book?" asked Mr. Mann.

"My own," she said.

"You could get someone to identify you?" he said.

A look of bewilderment swept over the face with the blue eyes.

"I shouldn't bring anyone else's," she said, revealing country simplicity. And the young man had felt the breath of the country sweep through the offices of the money lender.

"Could you get anyone to say you—"

"To say I'm me?" she said. "Well, there's Mrs. Smith."

"Smiths of Oak Houses?" asked the money-lender brightening. The girl shook her head. She mentioned an obscure a street in the poorest part of the town. Unable to stand it any longer the young man entered Mr. Man's office.

"It's all right," he said easily. "I'll go bail for this young lady. She's all right."

A pair of blue eyes flashed through tears.

"Right, Rennie," said Mr. Mann. He had great faith in his clerk's discretion, though there was something he did not understand about it. The girl had looked as surprised as Mr. Mann had felt. Rennie wasn't in the habit of knowing any young ladies.

With five pounds in her pocket, her bank book in Mr. Mann's charge, Mary Brierley went out of the money-lender's office. She went straight to the post office; got two postal orders, one for a pound, the other for two pounds, got two stamps, and on the way home groceries. Two pounds she sent to the workhouse on the hill for uncle John James' coffin, the other she sent to Annice, with a cheery letter that revealed nothing of her own difficulties.

What pleased her more than anything was the fact that she had got back the lucky sixpence, for 'Rennie' had remembered and given it to her just as she was leaving.

She wrote to Lucy saying that money had been sent for uncle's funeral, and hoped they would see that he was laid in the old churchyard at home. Lucy wrote back saying a pound would have been enough to send for a workhouse coffin such as he would be sent in, and telling her that of course, he would be buried from there now, and would she go to the funeral.

In borrowed black of Mrs. Smith's, Mary went to Lucy's to see the last of her old uncle.

"Why," she said, "what a fine coffin!"

"I can't understand it," said Lucy.

But they understood it soon afterwards. Uncle John James' lawyer informed the astonished relatives that the old man whom they have thought without a penny piece, and whom they had dispatched to the workhouse, had a pot of money in the safekeeping of a friend, and that whilst he had died in the workhouse hospital he had been well attended and content as a man of means. The writing of the authorities about the coffin was a dodge of the old man's, as he wished to leave his 'bit o' Brass' to that one of his family who paid for his coffin.

Mary Brierley came into a decent little sum of money, which, though not sufficient to keep her without employment altogether, placed her beyond the reach of care. But she insisted on going back to the town of her adoption—the great, new, strange town. She had several things to attend to, and besides as she said conclusively, she had on borrowed clothes.

****

Mary Brierley's first duty on returning to Crayton was to pay a visit to the money-lenders, and clear off the debt she owed Mr. Mann. In the course of a little chat with 'Rennie' she revealed the fact that she would like some semi-employment. Mr. Mann being called, the up-shot of it was that she was engaged to help in the growing work of correspondence.

But she did not remain long in her new office. 'Rennie' being promoted to the position of junior partner, he found her a new vocation, and to this day they count the beginning of their homely happiness from the date of the losing and finding of the lucky sixpence now set in a silver frame, and worn on 'high days and holidays' as a brooch.

Cotton Factory Times, August 4, 1916

Benny's love affair; his rival's ruse

Sammy, the blacksmith, looked up from shoeing the doctor's horse. Benny's shadow fell on the smithy floor.

"Well, owt fresh, Benny?" he asked.

"Aye," said Benny. There was a half smile in his eyes.

"Well," asked Sammy.

"She ta'en me," answered Benny, pushing his hands into his pockets with a satisfaction that nearly drove his rival wild.

"Well, I'm ——" he began.

It was all a mystery to him. He had though he knew all about women. Twice Benny's size, handsome, brainier, braver, and with the give of the gab, he had lost Milly Polson, a comely lass, with a hundred pounds ready money, to halting-tongued Benny, who some said was only elevenpence ha'penny to the shilling.

"However did that manage it?" asked Sammy.

Benny winked one eye, and was mum.

"Well," said Sammy, "if tha'll wait half-an-hour I'll be finished, an' we'll drink her health an' thine." Benny waited. It. was scarcely according to his precepts and ideas. But it was only once in a lifetime that he would be engaged to be married.

Inside the half-hour Sammy and Benny were seated in the "Blue Jug."

"I munnot stay more'n a quarter," said Benny. "I promised to meet Milly, an' go o'er Noggarth Tops wi' her."

Ho began to whistle the song that says,

"It's a starry night for a ramble,
Among the brush an' bramble."

Sammy vowed to himself that whatever happened, Bonny should not go over Noggarth Top that night.

"An old beer for Benny, and one for me." said Sammy. Benny's look was expostulation.

"Tha'd surely not drink th' health o' a lass like Milly i' milk?" asked the smith.

"Here's to th' health o' Milly an' Benny,"' said Sammy, "n' may Milly never got th' upper hand o' him."

"Amen!" said Benny, and took a spoonful of beer into his mouth, with the expression of a poisoned rat.

"Benny," said Sammy, lifting his glass, "what I don't know about horse shoes an' women isn't worth knowin'."

Benny nodded.

"There's three things to remember, wi' women. Th' first is, never let them see tha cares for 'em; th' second is, they like a chap can best 'em, like a dog does; th' last is, when tha's said a thing, stick to it, because that makes thee look to be depended on." Saying which Sammy emptied his glass, and rung the bell for more old beer for Benny and for himself.

"I'll remember them," said Benny. "No, no, Sammy. No mooar."

"I'll throw it on thi if tha doesn't, an' she'll smell it mooar if it's outside than in," said Sammy, seizing Benny's glass.

"Well, well, it's only once in a while." Said Benny, and began to empty his glass. A sparkle had begun to appear in his eye. He was squaring his shoulders, too. The somewhat timorous cast of his countenance was giving way to a benevolent pride in himself, Milly, and the world. Sammy's precepts, too, were ringing in his ears. He was going to show Milly that she wasn't taking a little boy. So she could wait for him. He began the second glass of beer. It didn't taste so bad, and the effect was even more courageous. Besides, she couldn't have waited long yet, and it wasn't raining.

"I think I'd better be goin'," he said, at last. "There's a sort o' fog comin' on, isn't there, Sammy?" Sammy had a smile.

"Just sit there a bit," he told Benny. "I'm getting some tobacco. Then I'll go out wi' thi." Benny nodded. The warmth from the inn fire was overpowering, and the queer fog in the room made him want to sleep. The landlord startled him.

"Benny," he said, "come on, let's ha' thee out."

"Eh!" gasped Benny.

"Turnin' eawt time," he said.

"I've to go o'er Noggarth," said Benny.

"Tha hasn't," grinned the landlord. "Sammy left word that he'd gone instead o' thee."

"I'm goin' o'er N'oggarth," reiterated Bennv. "I've said it, an' I'll stick to it." He was amazed at the new man he was become. Between the beer and the precept he fell fit to fight the world single-handed. He went along to Milly's, and knocked on the door, not very gently.

"Who's there?" asked a voice from the upper window, in the subdued tone proper to the neighbourhood, and the time of the night.

"It's me. I've come to take Milly o'er Noggarth," said Benny, firmly, "an' I'll not stir away fro' this door hoyle till she's donned up an' comes eawt."

"I'll do nowt o' th' sort," snapped Milly's voice. It sounded tearful, too. Benny began to sing and whistle, in the intervals asking if she'd got her hat on, as if these nocturnal ramblings were to be a regular feature of their courtship.

"Go down to him. Milly, and get him out o' the street." said Milly's gentle, respectable victim to the late Mr. Polson.

Milly dressed and went down, opening the street door softly. She had tossed a white shawl over her head.

"Oh, thar't ready," said Benny, seizing her by the arm.

"I've bin o'er Noggarth once, wi' my future husband, Sammy," she said. Her tone was enough to have frozen anyone but Benny in his exuberant state.

"I said we'd go o'er Noggarth to-neet," said Benny, ignoring the remark. "an' bein' a man o' my word, we're goin'. An' th' sooner we set out th' sooner we get back."

Milly stood against the doorstones, and would not budge an inch. Then Benny began to pay her compliments. Sho went a yard or two further to get him away from the windows of the Browns, inveterate gossips, and the natural enemies of the Polsons, because the Polsons' cat had once torn up nasturtians in their back window box.

After some time Mrs. Polson came down, opened the door gently, calling in a whisper "Has he gone, Milly?"

There was no answer but the wind along the dark streets. Benny, stubborn as a mule against releasing Milly's arm, had insisted on her going over Noggarth with him, and Milly's fear and the threat to rouse the village community if she did not obey him, had got her on the way. In the wind and the blackness, with the cold sound of water running through the night, Milly was dragged along by the man whom she had said "Yes" to, because as she told her mother, " I've known him a long a long time, and knew Benny wouldn't play his monkey tricks on me as my father did by you."

At two in the morning Benny brought her to her own door, saying "Now, that's number one in the programme. Good neet."

"Don't talk to me," said Milly, as her mother came with the candle. "I could kill Benny. That foo'l!"

She broke into sobs of rage.

Next day, in his shop, Benny received the following note:

—

Dear Mr. Smiles.- You may consider our engagement at an end. If you make any trouble Mr. Samuel Grimes will deal with you. — Yours truly,

Milicent Pelson.

The next evening he duly presented himself at the Pelsons. So soon as he stepped into the lighted kitchen he found Sammy sitting on the chintz-covered sofa, his arm around Milly's waist. He did not withdraw it as he saw Benny, but rather tightened his grip, nodding "Good evening, Benny". He hoped that Benny would withdraw, in very humiliation of soul. Benny did no such thing. He pulled out a cigarette, leaned back in the chair, and appeared ready to make a night of it, even asking if Milly couldn't find him anything like 'Comic Cuts' to pass the time on with. The scene was very different from that Milly had pictured, and such as she had seen in town theatres. Every courting night it became Benny's custom to drop in and sit there, talking to the couple.

One evening he did not appear. Milicent Pelson was fidgety that night, so much so that she quarrelled with Samuel, after which she sat glaring at the chair Benny had usually occupied, doling them out advice as to how to avoid squalls when they married.

Benny had carried out Samuel's "don't care" precept. It had a miraculous effect. When she saw him next morning in the street, she smiled. They drifted into conversation. Benny did not appear eager. He even broke off in a sentence to smile at a lilac-gowned female whom Milly told herself was at least thirty-five!

Besides, she had not found out where he had been last night.

"Benny," she said, and struggling with a rising blush, "I—I sort o' rued at bein' so hasty — "

Benny looked at her, looked at her with his old denseness.

"Oh, aye," he drawled.

He stopped there.

She had fled.

"Milly," he called behind her.

"Tell thi mother she can ha' that lobby cloth to th' trade, if she will. It's out o' date."

"Mother," said Milly, getting in. "Yo' can ha' that lobby cloth at trade rates. It's out o' date."

Mrs. Pelson stared at her daughter.

"I could kill Benny," she repeated, with greater fervour than ever. He's such a foo'! But I wonder——"

She broke into tears.

Whereupon Mrs. Pelson reminded Milly of the parable of the dog with the meat that lost it for a shadow.

The next day it was rumoured all over the village that Benny was going to be married. He was having a new shop front put in, and the place "done through".

"Tha'a missed a bargain," said Mrs. Pelson. "Benny was that overjoyed that night he got a little—well, too much. There's summat I like about Benny, though he's more overbearing than one would think a little quiet chap could be. But it shows he's a back bone, an' he seems to be comin' out all ways. I wonder who she is."

Milly went, somewhat draggled looking, to the smithy.

"Samuel," she said, haltingly, "I sort o' rued — "

He glared at her blushes, angrily.

"I know,' he said. "It's all o'er th' village. I knew tha'd ha' him. Well, I wish yo' luck. For my part, tha'rt too changeable for me, Milicent Pelson, an' I've pick'd up with a woman settled in character, so I'm not wearing the willow about thee an' Benny."

Milly stared, then tumbled.

She broke into hysterical laughter and left the smithy. Till then she had hardly known whether she liked Benny or Sammy most. Benny had been showing her what he could do if he liked.

She met him outside, smoking a cigar.

"Come an' see th' shop front," he said, in his quiet voice. We'll get all the custom in the village, Milly. It's IT. An' th' parlour's fit for a queen to sit in. By the way, I've put th' banns up, an' we'll ha' a quiet wedding — with no 'strong drink.' Though I mun say it's sort o' made me get a move on—given me a start like."

"Where did tha go that night tha didn't come?" asked Milly, almost bursting with curiosity.

"I walked reawnd an' reawnd th' houses, wanting to punch Sammy's head." said Benny. "An' I noticed th' shadows weren't so lovin'. I've got to thank Sammy for some advice he gave, though. It was good advice. I feel like a chap 'at has mastered his pair o' lions. There's nothing I can't do now."

Samuel Grimes got his match in the woman of "settled character". The story of their domestic upheavals was the meat for village gossips leaning on their brooms. Mrs. Smiles would talk of it, too. She had found Benny more tractable as husband than she had found him as lover— but the memory of that night when he had dragged her o'er Noggarth made her always look on him as something not quite a fool.

Cotton Factory Times, December 15, 1916

Nanny's bad fortune: the stolen pluck

"How we're going to manage through th' week-end I don't know," sighed Nanny's married daughter, who had come home to live again, with her two bairns, after a half-dozen years of unhappy married life. "If I hadn't been here, yo' could ha' had money for your rooms."

She began to cry.

She was off work with neuritis.

"Shut thi daft face," said Nanny, cheerfully. "An' as for managin' through a week-end, well, I've managed through my time, somehow, an' we can't stop at a week-end." She was a shadow-thin woman, with a pair of blue eyes glinting through steel-rimmed glasses that lent the little face an owlish look.

"Sitha! Look at that," she exclaimed, triumphantly, "an' say if I haven't missed my way i' life. I should ha' bin a Paris hat trimmer. I should ha' bin lots of things, but oather they missed me or I missed them, than on't. But then, if lots had had my hard life they'd ha' bin i' th' 'sylum, so I allus look on it I'd sooner ha' it than them, and them be drivin' to th' 'sylum. I sort o' feel I've saved 'em summat."

She turned her bonnet round and round admiringly. At every turn she recognised some relic. The steel buckle had been on Jenny's dancing shoes. Jenny had been her favourite child. She had gone off into a weakness. There was the purple velvet that had been one of her dress sleeves in the days when the sun had shone on her for a little, when the despondent woman now groaning over her sorrows, had been at home, and earning good money. She stroked it with a toil-worn finger tenderly. Even Abe, her dead husband, had liked that frock, though he usually hardly knew if she wore velvet or sacking. The bit of lace had been a tie given to her by Ben, now out in Salonika. Poor Ben! How he loved a pork pie!

"How's it look, Mary?" she asked, fixing it, and looking anxiously at her daughter.

"My Sunda' hat is a shame to be seen," said Mary. "Do you think, mother—"

"Of course I can," said Nanny, her face lighting up. Mary had indeed paid her hat trimming a compliment. She had invited her mother's help to that old hat of hers.

"Dare you wash the feathers?" queried Mary.

"Dare I?" laughed Nanny. "I dare do owt. That's how I've getten through. Aye, marry, I dare. Now I mun put it away."

"Here's a beggar," said Mary, from her seat by the window. "Don't give her owt, mother."

"No," said Nanny and went to the door.

In the end she came back and went to the drawer.

"A ha'penny won't make or break us," she said, apologetically.

Mary sniffed.

Then she heard her mother's firm reply as she was asked for old stockings.

"Bless you, missus, we darn 'em up till they're fit for th' museum. If we didn't I couldn't ha' gan yo' that ha'penny," sounded the fresh voice. "I'm thinking a day may come when I've to go round wi' a basket misel' but I shouldn't like to. It's such a poor quality o' thread."

Then she came in and got ready to go out and spend the two and sixpence that was to get in food for three days. With shining face, her new-old bonnet, and string bag, and the boots that she only wore on high days and holidays because they pinched her bunion, she set out. She had put a good face on that two and six problem to Mary, but there was a quaking in her heart. Tom, her crippled lad, was fond of something tasty. If he didn't get it there would be a cloud over the house. Taking papers round in the rain was dree work, poor lad, and his temper was melancholy. Nanny had to strike a cheerful note on account of the rest of her family. It had grown to be real to her, but sometimes—

Two-and-sixpence.

She was meditating, and almost collided with a fat old man.

"Good morning, Mrs. Gray," he said.

"Good morning, Mr. Holmes," replied Nanny.

"Have you seen th' paper this mornin'?" he asked.

Nanny whitened and gasped.

"Ben," she began.

"He's got promoted," said Ned Holmes.

Nanny was panting, white still, but managing a smile.

"Have you thought about what I asked," enquired Ned.

"I'm not of marrying age," said Nanny; "and anyhow, I never mean to get married, so don't ask me again."

This was the usual rigmarole.

"I'll never ask thee again, Nanny, never," said Ned. "There's no nonsense about me. I've only thought o' thee strugglin' among it. An'—but never mind. Aye, Nanny, I like thee because tha'rt such a rare plucked 'un."

He laughed and passed on.

Nanny looked after him.

"A rare plucked 'un!" If he only knew! If he only knew how the bitter struggle to live was becoming almost too much for her, so that she could scarcely sleep o' nights, and when she did it was to dream of losing her old purse that never had much in, or of Ben being killed, or of Mary crying. She had had 60 years of it, hoping against hope— putting that cheerful face up to the world's limelight, when she had to laugh to keep from crying.

She paused before a butcher's window.

It was as she had thought. All the things she had wanted were gone, and she would have to go to town. She half thought of a car, but a car cost a penny. She might be just a penny short, so she didn't speculate. The village woman trudged away through the streets, occasionally peeping into a shop window. There were hats at a sovereign each. Good gracious! Her whole outfit had never had to cost more than that. It must be grand to be able to walk into a place, and just pop things on. Then she started. Something must be the matter with her to be thinking this way on. The pluck was going out of her. She felt panicky. If that went — She smiled wearily.

Before a large, prosperous-looking shop she paused. The greedy feeling that had been hers before the hat shop came back. Red polony, yellow cheese, new butter, fresh eggs.

Hadn't she been toiling all her life, always going a little short, always counting the potatoes, always starving half a week after the Christmas feast. Then she shook herself. It was the devil muttering to her.

She went into the shop.

A smart young woman came to attend to her.

"Han yo' got a nice pluck?" asked Nanny.

"Yes," answered the young woman.

"I'll see it," said Nanny, leaving her basket against the counter.

It was a nice pluck.

"Tenpence," the young woman told her.

"I'll take it," said Nanny, hiding jubilation behind a quiet voice.

"Ten per pound," said the young woman.

"Oh!"

Nanny's face had fallen.

"Weigh it," she said. If she only had enough to get it! There would be stew, broth, liver for one day, pluck pie for another, and Ben's pay would have arrived then.

"Two pounds."

"And how much is th' head," asked Nanny, critically examining it with her eyes.

"Sixpence!"

It just left her twopence for the gas.

She drew a breath of relief.

"I'll have it," she said.

The earth was firm under her feet again. Mary would not cry, her crippled boy would be good tempered, and—well, she felt like something tasty herself. Perhaps she was run down or something. The kettle had felt heavy lately.

The young woman went behind a quarter of a cow to wrap it up. She was a long time, Nanny thought. The new-old bonnet bobbed about as Nanny tried to see. At last she got the right angle for observation.

Her cheeks flushed with indignation.

"I only want one pluck," she said, trying to be charitable. They were trying to rob her, because she was not so rich as the fancy woman with the furs who had ordered two pounds of butter sending by the boy.

"I know," said the town woman, politely.

Nanny waited until she brought the pluck. She tried to wrap it up so that Nanny would not see it.

"I'll take that I paid for," she said. Something was stirring in her that amazed her. That woman was trying to dodge her, because she was poor, and looked simple and quiet. Somehow or other something had been dodging her all her life.

She stood erect.

She was fighting for those at home.

"They are both alike," said the young woman.

"There's no need to change 'em then," said Nanny, with great sarcasm. She had seen the ram's head to which this pluck had been attached. Noah might have had that ram in the ark.

The young woman reddened.

She went to get the other pluck.

"An' I'll tak' th' leets, too," said Nanny, "sin' I've paid for them."

There was restrained anger in her voice.

As the parcel was made up Nanny said, "I may be cabbage-lookin', miss, but I'm not green."

Taking her twopence she went out of the shop.

When she had got away she sure that the blood was dripping through her basket. Not even enough paper for the poor, who carried their own stuff.

She set it down to arrange it, or try to.

Just then she saw a car coming, and just in front of it a lonely kitten.

Nanny shut her eyes.

"I knew it!" she said.

Then she opened them, and saw the kitten was safe, pushed along by the guard.

"Silly thing!" she murmured.

She turned to her basket.

Alas!

Some yards away a dog had trailed out that which she had fought for, planned about, schemed and already cooked, in her mind's eye.

A dry sob came into her throat.

She picked up a stone, and then stared in dumb horror. It had gone through a shop window. The dog was trailing the pluck away. The shopman came out.

"Aye, it were me. I were sendin' it at the dog as stole my stuff," said Nanny. "But yo' can't draw blood from a stoan, an' yo' can't make folk pay as has nowt, can you? An' I don't care. Send me to prison if yo' like. 'T won't be much worse."

The man was staring at her in amazement.

Something gleamed in his eyes—an understanding of the old fashioned figure with the shadow-thin face.

"It's all right," he said. "It's insured."

Then he said, "What the trouble?"

"I've lost my pluck," said Nanny, brokenly. "I can't face 'em without dinner. I can't it, mister."

She began to trail away.

"Here," he called.

"No," said Nanny, stubbornly. "I never accept charity."

"Good morning," he said, and went within.

"Jimmy," he said to the shary lad, "there's an old woman in the queerest bonnet thou'll meet on the street. Run down th' back streets and get in front o' her, and drop this half sovereign, an' see she finds it, an' I'll gie thee a free ticket for th' cinema and a night off."

The lad ran after Nanny.

He returned soon afterwards.

"She picked it up," he said, "an' she asked me if it were mine, and she nearly made me ha' it, but when I said it would be wrong because it weren't mine and she'd found it, she nearly set off on th' run."

"She'll ha' found her pluck," he said.

****

Two weeks later Ned Holmes died, leaving all his worldly possessions to Nanny, who had refused him times innumerable. The shock of finding herself secure put Nanny into bed. She said faintly to Mary, "Well, we can afford to be ill if we like now. An' money's very useful when th' pluck is done."

Cotton Factory Times, March 9, 1917

'Lijah and Nancy and the beech tree

Every morning when Nancy wound up the little blind the tree, full of birds chattering for their breakfast, met her eyes. Every day as the sun dropped, Elijah grumbled, and threatened to cut it down, as it "shut th' leet off his paper".

"If ever tha cuts that tree down, 'Lijah," she would tell him, "thee an' me goes each our own way.'"

It was a curious bit of psychology that she, who had stood the storm rack of life with Elijah for nigh on fifty years—she who had felt the strength of his arm, though not for her, but against her, she whom he had railed at in adversity and shut out in prosperity, should have that flash in her eye, that determination to leave Elijah for ever, if he harmed that tree in their front garden. Elijah would sit and stare at it sulkily, as the only thing Nancy had really opposed him in. With his lame foot on a buffet, he would glare at it as if the trembling beech were some human that wronged him.

"Shakin an' shiverin' i' th' wind enough to chill anybody's blood," he would say. "I wish thou'd to sleep down here an' hear it half o' th' neet. 'Tis waur nor th' pain i' my leg. But thou never had no feelin' for me, Nancy."

"If I'd none 'tis twice as much as ever thou had for me," his wife would answer.

"Well, fill my pot," he would retort. "'Tis nigh empty. Thou'll not be troubled wi' mi' lung. An' tha'rt ten years younger than me, an' not bad lookin'."

Nancy would then trot off with the jug, for ale to fill the pot that ever stood waiting on the shining stand inside the fender. She did not like to hear him talk of his approaching end. But sometimes, when he was unusually nettlesome, she would pop on her bonnet, go out, and stay out a few hours. She invariably returned looking buoyed up as with some new hope.

It was in vain that Elijah tried to find out where she had been. Always, after those visits to the unknown, he was more bitter against the tree that darkened the window. It was his way of getting even with her. He could not punch her head, now, as in the days of his virile manhood. He had degenerated. He was 'going into eighty'. Nancy was quite young, being only seventy, and he knew that if he hopped out of life she would be sure to wed again. Joe Giles was living yet, the man of whom she had always said she could have wiped her feet on him and he'd have kissed them.

But more and more as he listened to the beech he suspected that Joe Giles was waiting for him to "kick the bucket," when he and Nancy could be very comfortable on his, Elijah's, burial insurance, Joe's rent from one house, and their united old age pensions.

One day a trap stopped before their door. Joe Giles stepped out of it.

"Come in," Elijah heard Nancy say, in a fluttering, pleased way.

Joe came in.

The young demon had on a straw hat, and actually did not look a day older than sixty.

"Hale an' hearty," he laughed, in answer to Nancy's inquiry after his health. "Likely for livin' to a hundred, an' wouldn't mind reaching to a thousand; providin' I could get enough to eat. Aye! It's a fine world, 'Lijah, so lung as we con stick on us pins, an' see out o' our eyes, an' eat home-made bread. I say, let's do it."

"Ay! Ay!" said Elijah, stroking his beard.

Strange thoughts, dark thoughts, were moving in his mind. Joe had come to crow over his ill-health, and physical dependence on Nancy. And why had Nancy put on her clean Sunday apron that afternoon? It was Joe Giles she went to see on those days when he was cantankerous — Joe Giles, who had always been one of the genial, light ones.

"Stop to a dish o' tay," invited Nancy.

"Ay,' mumbled Elijah. Joe took off his hat, and set it on Nancy's best pot dogs on the dresser. Joe was full of old memories over the tea. Nancy actually laughed, a quavering, hesitant laugh, like a sweet note on a shaking fiddle string.

After tea Joe said he'd enjoyed himself mightily, and would like to come again. He'd been a sort of lonesome since Susan died. A man was only half a man without a woman to protect him.

"Soa tender they are," he said eulogising his dead wife, "so keerful that a mon doean't hurt hissel'. Ay! Ay!"

Before he went he sang them a song about somebody donning an old straw bonnet with red ribbons and riding over clover fields to Dover on her golden wedding day. Elijah caught a look that passed between Nancy and Joe, as the latter stood on the mat. It was an encouraging look Joe gave as much as to say, "All's well, and couldn't be better." Nancy's was beseeching. Then the door dosed, the horse trotted off, and Nancy came in and sat down to her knitting of a new pair of socks for Elijah.

The old man sat brooding.

Nancy went upstairs to bed. Elijah could not bear anyone tossing beside him when the pain was in his leg.

As he lay watching his shadow on the white blind the candle fluttering in the wind as it stood by his four poster bed with the very coverlet that had been made by Nancy in their courting days, he heard the beech in the garden outside. It was laughing at him. He was sure of it. It started low down, and gradually grew bolder, laughing out loud, and as he listened to it, the secret of Nancy's love for that tree was made clear to him. The Giles' had possessed a beech in their garden, when Nancy and Joe were young, and when she had answered "No". She loved it for all that might have been.

Putting on his socks Elijah Mason got out of bed. He was lamer than ever, because excited, he cursed the beech laughing outside in the dark, from its furthest root to its topmost branch. He was going to chop it down. Always it had seemed to stand between the light and him. He knew now why that was. It stood for an old tender memory of Joe, in Nancy's mind. In the morning it would be gone.

He dressed, creeping about cautiously, but inadvertently kicked the coal bucket. He forgot the pain in his foot and leg. He was only afraid Nancy would hear him.

At last he found the axe.

Noiselessly unlocking the door, he stole out into the darkness. The beech was making the same tantalising sound. Elijah laughed, too, but there was murder in the mumble of it. They had thought to be riding in that trap when Nancy's golden wedding day came round. He crept near to the bench, with upraised axe. Thien, as if in expostulation he heard a cry from that upper room, where Nancy's candle yet burnt.

"'Lijah! 'Lijah!"

He imagined that she was watching him from the window and smote savagely at the beech.

"'Lijah!" moaned nancy.

"I'll chop it down, and thou leaves me to the streets," said 'Lijah. "An' when I've done wi' it, I'll make sure there's no golden weddin' day for thee."

Destruction was raging in his mind. Was it his fault that he had been born morose and treating that worst he loved best, to hide his affection? Poverty, too, had irritated him as a red rag a bull. But he had cared for Nancy, who was now building on living in peace with Joe when he was in his grave. She had asked Joe to come and see him to see if he would last much longer, and Joe had bidden her be of good heart, with that look of his, saying "all was well". It was true he had sometimes punched Nancy's head, as a fetish for a dull life. But she—she had broken his heart, as he stood on the brink of the grave. Chop—choppety—chop!

He was striking at the beech now.

In the intervals he heard Nancy moaning his name. But he went on with his task. At last he felt the beech sway. The work became a passion to him; then, yet still the leaves laughed on. But soon they would be hushed. Then—he would deal with Nancy.

"Crash!"

The beech came down upon the garden, barely missing Elijah. It would never laugh again; the birds would never sing there again; Nancy would never stand in the doorway, looking at it because it reminded her of Joe, and that Elijah was ten years older. She would never give it that proud little nod, as she went out, on one of those mysterious

visits. She would never go on those mysterious visits again
— because! —

He began to tear up the sods around it, as if to separate
the vitality of the living earth with the pitiful stump that
remained. His hand struck something hard. He scraped
like a ferret, and as wildly, in the dark. A tin box came to
his grasp. He took it into the house, opened it. Letters! Love
letters! For they were tied with blue ribbons. He looked at
the axe, shining in the candle light. First he would read.

Then, he started.

For there, ghost-like in the candle light, were the pale
letters of words he himself had written to Nancy, when
struggle had never touched them. He had bidden her burn
them, but she had buried them. One by one he drew them
out. How many times he had said he would make her happy!
His hand began to shake, his heart began to tremble, like
one fronting old ghosts of youth, as he stood on the brink
of the grave. Then, the last drawn away, he started back
again. A scrap of paper was amongst it. He opened it.

"For 'Lijah, when I am gone," he read. "I never rued,
'Lijah, I liked the beech for the letters, 'Lijah." There were
other words, but he did not read. He had always thought
she wanted him gone, conscious of his own shortcomings.

"'Lijah!" he heard, from above.

He began to trail himself up those stairs on his hands
and knees.

When he reached the top stair he heard Nancy panting.
She motioned him to raise her up.

"The beech!" she gasped. "The beech, 'Lijah dig" —

Her lips were blue.

Elijah began to curse. She was going to die. He shook
her gently.

"Nancy Langston." He said, giving her her youthful
maiden name. "I don't want it, the brass, Nancy — "

He nearly ran down and upstairs again with brandy.

In two minutes she was coming round.

"Joe Giles said thou'd outlive me, at th' door," she said,
half consciously. "But I've allus bin feared tha wouldn't."

Bit by bit he got the truth. Whenever he had been ill-
tempered she had looked on it as an illness, and had

consulted numerous spiritualists on the subject. They all affirmed Elijah would see her put in the ground. The hours she had spent away from home had been passed in this manner, and by cleaning for folk and putting the money under the beech for Elijah.

On their golden wedding day Elijah and Nancy startled the natives by riding out in Joe Giles' trap to the scene of their early youth.

"The happiest woman on God's green earth, just as thou said tha'd make me," wagged Nancy, as the bells jingled.

Elijah scratched his head, and thanked God that he made fools to protect other fools from their opinions of themselves.

Cotton Factory Times, June 1, 1917

Sarah's chap and her people

The little house winked with its Saturday night brightness. The chairs had their week-end covers on; the sewing machine, on which Sarah had that week made herself a grand new blouse, was decorated by the white box cover and the fern-pot, that reflected in its brass side the light of the chandelier. Ned looked across at his wife, Betty, who was knitting her boy, Ben, a pair of socks.

"We'll look varra weel—when we've cleyned up, lass," he remarked. Betty and he matched the chintz-covers on the chairs, but not the brass fern-pot. That was Sarah's idea. And odd things in the kitchen thus contradicted each other—the old Lancashire of the parents, and the new Lancashire of the girl. The lads were easy-going and rough and ready, like Betty and Ned. But the girl read, did fancy work, and had studied grammar. She was out now.

"I don't know," said Betty, straightening her shoulders shawl. "It depends on what *he* thinks."

Ned stared as if his 'old rib' had gone demented.

"Our Sarah's courtin'," his wife told him, not giving him time to speak.

"Our Sarah!" He gasped. Then his face became one big question mark.

"Nay!" replied Betty. "I don't know. All I know is he comes miles fro' here, an' he wear a gowd hoop.. An' she's axed me to ax thee an' th' lads not to talk soa broad to-morn at tay-time when he's here. An' she's hinted that you'd look seemlier in a collar, dad, an' that you might scrape th' muck off your shoon after you've fed the hens."

Ned leaned on his chair-arm.

His face would have been a goldmine to a film company for the time.

"Yo' bring them up, and toil an' moil, an' lie awaken when they cut their teeth," he said, meditatively, "an' then they ax yo' to be put in a collar—because of a young calf in a gowd hoop."

"Say nowt ower the gowd hoop," said Betty "It weren't Sarah told me over it. But I thinks to mysel', "Sara, lass, thy father an' me got on very nicely, an' he'd no gowd hoop!"

There was strong prejudice, the prejudice of the plain old Lancashire folk, in her tone. It was reflected in Ned's face as in a mirror.

The front door flew open just at this point. Sarah Cherry entered, a comely, intelligent looking girl, typical of the new Lancashire, with its half-scorn of the old, broad tongue, of porridge, and homespun.

She inquired after food-stuffs for the morrow's tea with a pretty anxiety. Seeing all that was in, nothing forgotten, she dashed out again.

"I wish he'd had owt but a gowd hoop," said Ned, sucking at his pipe.

Next morning the two women were at it early.

Ben came creeping into the kitchen to stare at the piled-up table.

Sarah was making bed upstairs.

"Our Sarah's chap's comin'," his mother told him. "So thee an' th' others want to get a' your silly talk out o' you before he lands. He's a sort o' th' better end o' th' working class, an' he wears a gowd hoop."

Ben stared, then rapped out the 'National Anthem' on his jaw bone, as was customary when he was either amused or excited.

The fact that Sarah's chap was coming, and that they must be on their best behaviour, went round to her brothers, particularly that he wore a gold hoop.

Consequently at three o'clock prompt, Will Gray stepped into an atmosphere correct and cool as an ice refrigerator. At tea-time nobody joked. All the conversation seemed have made up of "yes's" and "no's", "pleases's" and "thank you's" and the meal seemed to last an eternity. Betty had on her silk dress that she had not worn for years. Ned was collared. The lads were always decent. But they did not dare open their mouths. The had been warned not to show their ignorance.

When Will had gone with Sarah it was like a spell breaking.

"There's summat sly an' underneath about him," was Betty's verdict. "An' I saw him eyein' a' th' stuff—fair snighin' his nose at it, like. An' he hardly ate aught. An' I heard him say to our Sarah in th' lobby, 'Let's get out of this, Sarah'."

Ben, Tom, and Harry liked him no more than their parents did.

"Did you see how he looked at dad when he pu'd pipe out?" said Tom. "He doesn't smoke, I'll warrant. He fair looked like he couldn't abide it."

During the next week Sarah had much to say on the virtues of her young man.

"Is he comin' to tea again?" asked Ben.

So that was the reason Ben went out.

The same sort of atmosphere of prevailed again. The only person in the house, apart from Sarah, who got near to the intruder was the cat. It sprung on the back of Will Gray's chair, to Betty's horror of such familiarity. She "clouted" it, out of form, but hated the lad with the gold hoop for having been the cause.

As for Sarah, she was getting out of bounds.

None of her clothes were good enough to wear, and she was forever pulling at Betty to get her new ones.

"I'd get no more clothes till he axed me back to my tea, if I were thee," said Betty, aggravated out of patience. "He wears a gowd hoop, but doesn't know much manners. I read it in t' paper under 'The Lady's Lines' that he should have had thee to see his folk."

Mother and daughter stared into each other's eyes.

To Betty's infinite horror and pain Sarah, swanky little Sarah, hard little Sarah, the apple of her mother's eye, burst into tears.

She had touched the sore spot in the girl's heart.

"I've axed him, and he's put me off," she sobbed. "So I thought if I got some clothes—" She had dropped into dialect in her excitement.

"If it's clothes that's stoppin' him introducin' thee to his famly," vowed Betty, "I'll see tha has some."

That very week Sara got a new rig-out, and Betty and Ned brightened to see Sarah get lighter hearted. But it did not last long.

"Where does he live?" asked Ned.

"You're neither o' yo' goin'—where you're not wanted. Nor me either," she said, with sudden determination. Ned and Betty both realized that Sarah was theirs—of their spirit, if not of their letter, at that moment. So Sarah Cherry wrote a letter to Will Gray, sending it to the house she had never seen, the house with a high-sounding name.

"Dear Mr. Gray (it ran)—I am writing to break off her engagement, hoping it won't cause any pain.— (Snuffle, with the dull perception that it is the biggest lie she ever told.) I have been aware for some time that there is a barrier between us—that you are evidently ashamed of asking me to your house, and of introducing me to your people. I won't be engaged to be married to a man who's ashamed of owning me—(Gulp—gulp—with the clutch at her pride.) My parents quite agree with me in this.

—Yours truly, *Sarah Cherry.*"

A day or two went past. Ned and Betty watched Sarah pining. No letter came. The girl had gone to bed early one night, when Betty donned herself up in her best, and set off to the address she had copied from Sarah's letter to Gray as it had stood on the dresser, waiting for a stamp.

"We'll both go," said Ned, and got himself ready.

The tramcar took them near the place—near the road it mentioned. At last, after many inquiries, they came to the house of the high-sounding name. It was a ramshackle, half-ruined cottage, looking as if a gust of wind would blow it away. The lad of the gold hoop himself opened the door to them.

"Come in," he said, with a gesture that had in it a strange pride. They entered. It was a shabby kitchen. By the hearth sat an old woman—blind, as they saw.

"Bill," she said, "who's these?", feeling that strangers had entered the room.

"Friends," said the lad.

He still wore the gold hoop, conspicuous in the drab surroundings. His speech was grammatical, as on his visit to Sarah's house. But he wore old clothes, and his hands were grimy from an attempt to brighten the fender. A book was open on the table; a pipe was on the hob.

"Aye, friends," said Ned, hurriedly.

He was quicker than Betty to receive impressions. The lad of the gold hoop was near Ned's heart now."

"I'm glad tha's some, Bill," said the old woman. "I'll soon need none. An' no lad deserved 'em more—no lad."

Will tried to stop her, but she would not be stopped. The whole tale came out. It was very simple. Will Gray had been put into her arms at a railway station to 'hold a minute'—and never claimed. She had brought him up. The gold hoop was tied round his neck, but, unlike the stories, there was nothing but a plain ring that might be a ..

[The newspaper column ends here, with the text "Continued in Next Column" which starts a new paragraph...]

Will had worked for his foster mother these seven years, bringing her good wages from the coalpit. Reading he had always loved. Somehow or other he had met Sarah, got fond of her, but her ultra-respectability had overawed him. He had come to see her hoping to find she belonged to homely folk, but when he had come into the stiffness of the family could not ask them back to his home. For that shabby home, that old figure by the hearth, was his home. This latter all came out after the death of his foster mother, which happened two weeks later.

Sarah was glad to have Will Gray's confessions.

She had had such a taste of what it felt to be looked down on—or to imagine herself looked down on—that she was really relieved he had "no edge on him". Besides, Will Gray was, in Ned's own words, "a reight nice lad!"

Cotton Factory Times, July 6, 1917

The broken spell: a tale of by-gone days

Helen o' Jake's sat down to her breakfast, wondering at the unusual silence of her parents.

Jake Brown generally had some grumble over his food, whilst his buxom wife's tongue clattered forty miles an hour.

Jake was shovelling his porridge down without comment. Molly looked scared into speechlessness. Then bang came Jake's big fist on the farmhouse table.

"We're witched, by th' mass we are!" he exclaimed. "But I'll go off to Preston to see a wise man today."

He was soon ready by the aid of his wife and daughter. Mounted on his grey mare, Meg, he made the sparks fly from the cobbles of the main street as he clattered over them. Molly, meanwhile, had taken a Demonology book from the shelf, and was engrossed in it, occasionally calling on her saints.

"All th' bolts an' bars were undone when thy father came down this morn," said she to Helen. "We're witched! An' why should that sound beast die at Michaelmas? An' thee—thou's looked pined these days. Thy father an' me ha' noticed."

The beautiful face paled and flushed under her mother's glance. Nell Hill had changed these months. But the spell she was under was no old hag's — but Dan Cupid's. He had shot his arrows at her as she had looked from her aunt's bedroom windows in Rochdale to see the rushbearing cart with the king of the fete stood within the crown of flowers — the dizzy crown that topped a stck of rushes fifteen foot high.

Again as her mother spoke Nell saw the handsome dark-haired lad, with his merry eyes that had melted into a start of wonder as they had met her countenance looking into his from the window of the black and white timbered house. She had thrown him a garland. His eyes had said "Come" but her aunt had taken turn a turn for the worse, and dancing on the green for Nell had been impossible.

"She's witched, too." said Molly, as her daughter turned restlessly out at the white gate.

It was late when Jake returned from his visit to the wise man.

"We're witched," he said, heavily. "It's an old woman, with a mole and an ash stick. Boil those herbs at the stroke o' twelve, and — I know what to say. She'll pass o'er th' house mutterin', but she'll try agen. Aye, there's an ill spell woven ower Robin's Farm!"

Molly brought out a pot to hang over the fire to boil the herbs. Nell, who had been about to go to bed, shivered a little, and set down her candle. It was just about this moment that a man's voice sounded from the darkness outside.

"Which way to Nab's-road?" he asked. "I'm lost. Open the door, good Christians, and tell me the way."

"Through Pennel Forrest, said Jake, suspicion in look and voice. "It's on the left."

"My lantern's out," said the voice, in a rollicking way. "Give me a leet to see the witches by!"

"Open the door, father," said Nell.

"Decent folk are not about at this hour," said Jake.

"Nor up, either," said the young man's voice.

With some reluctance Jake opened the door.

The luminance streamed on a handsome stripling who had evidently imbibed too much ale. He entered the farm, got his lantern aglow and was about to depart when he caught sight of Nell. His exclamation made Molly and Jake regard the girl. Her face had whitened, her eyes shone, she was evidently under the spell of some great excitement.

"What ails thee, lass?" said Jake, giving her shoulder a shake.

"Leave her alone," said the young man. "Naught ails her. She threw me a garland at the rushbearing, that's all. The may's in my shoe to preserve me against witches."

It was just at this moment that the potion in the pan began to bubble, and Jake rushed to the door, locking it, saying, "It's twelve," and took from his pocket a paper.

"Stir it round, Molly," he said, head on one side.

"Father thinks we're witched." said Nell, aside.

"I'm sure I am," said the stripling, boldly.

Nell blushed.

"Round and round and round," said Jake, directing Molly. "Now—is th' smoke blue?"

He started the incantation. It was made up of strange things like 'Gabora, Gabora, gab,' and a school child of to-day would have laughed at it. But as the wind blew an extra loud gust a very shower of soot fell in the pan, turning all pale.

Nell's hand met the protecting clasp of the young king of the rushbearing. Looking up, Jake saw them.

"Get out, tha's broken th' spell," he stamped. "An' Nell — what's come ower thee?" For Nell, the proudest lass on Pendle side, had allowed a stranger to hold her hand.

"I shall come again," said the stripling, with a meaning look at Nell. Jake flew after him, but was too late. The door had been unlocked and locked again that chase was in vain. Moreover, the key was on the window-sill on the outside. The marlocking youth had locked Jake in his house.

For two minutes Jake stared. Then he said hollowly, "I'm none going to bed this neet. That lad's i' league with the witch. She's broken my spell by sending him — and he's putten the key ready for her." He settled himself for the night.

The two trembling women stole off upstairs. "I don't believe it," said Nell, suddenly. "An' there's folk leavin' off believin' i' witches. We're cowards — an' we get scared, an' if things go ill with men through their own neglect of their farms, or by chance — they lay it on some poor woman."

Love, the primitive, was combating the less ancient passion of superstition.

"Don't blaspheme," said her mother, crossing herself.

In the morning when they got up they found Jake asleep in the chair. All the doors were wide to the morning air. He stood stupefied when they told him what happened. Fear gripped all their hearts. The devil and his beldames must have unlocked that door. The key was still on the sill.

Again, Jake set off to see the wise man. When it got after twelve they got alarmed at his not returning.

"Set him the light in the window," said Nell. "It's dark crossing the tops."

"'t will draw the witches," said Molly, quavering.

"Is the devil stronger than the Lord?" asked Nell, bravely, and set the crucifix by the lamp.

They sat for some time by the fire. The silence — that silence of terror, with the man gone from the house, was terrible. Their heart-beats made great heavy strokes in between the tick of the case clock. Something thumped against the door — a stick tapped.

"Lord have mercy on us!" gasped Molly, and fainted.

"Who's there?" asked Nell.

Her knees were ashake under her.

A low moan from behind that closed door was the only answer.

"Speak your name, and I'll open to you," said the girl. "Who's your master?"

There was a rumble of thunder, a flash of vivid lightning in the black night, and Nell gave a half-scream. This was the witches' chorus. But the moan of speechless pain went on at the door. Torn between fear and sympathy, the girl rushed to the crucifix, and, holding it before before her, unlocked the door, throwing it open. A huddled body fell into the room. Molly opened her eyes.

"Jake!" she screamed. "Jake!"

Jake it was, a great gash over his eye.

In the morning he told the tale. He had been waylaid by robbers, beaten, and rescued by the young man of Nell's rush-bearing incident. But coming alone over the top giddiness had seized him, though he had assured Will hours before he was not much hurt, and could travel alone. But for the lamp in the window he would have broken his neck. Whilst, if Nell had not opened the door —

Wind and the storm, winch had not yet abated, made mother and daughter shudder for what fear might have made them do. In a while Jake took Molly and Nell to see Will Forest, and Jake's suspicion died — for ever. For it was Nell who discovered that her mother was a sleepwalker, and that it must have been she who let out the cattle every morning. She must have gone by the back way after Will locked them all in, opened the front door, laying the key back on the sill so noiselessly that she did not even awaken Jake. He made a point of fastening her wrist to his afterwards, to prevent Molly being taken for a witch, for he had somehow gleaned an idea of sleep-walking, and feared lest his own wife be taken for a witch.

When the reaction set in against the destroying of supposed witches, Jake himself was a missionary of light in the village, remembering that but for Nell's courage he would have died in the storm.

But Will Forest swore Nell put a spell on him as she threw her garland, and always said to the end of his life that it was never quite broken.

Cotton Factory Times, August 24, 1917

Corner Shops: the miracle

Three Bridges said that Jonathan Peel was killing his wife, Mary. But Three Bridges, regardless of its own verdict, went on eating the cakes she baked in the oven Doctor Mitchells said was burning her life away. There was a rumour that the old doctor had openly told Peel that though he could not be hung for it, he was driving nails in his wife's coffin.

Meanwhile, quite unconscious of this, bright-haired Miriam Peel wrote home gay and tender letters such as can only be written by youth — the untried — from the provincial college, where she was studying for her teaching certificate.

When she came home on the vacation before her examination her coming down the street towards the shop was watched by many eyes.

"She could gi'e her mother a bit o' fat an be noan the worse for it," said Nan Briggs, putting the sentiments of the watchers.

As she drew nearer a look of disappointment crept into those eyes. For weeks she had dreamed of this home-coming — picturing her mother in the doorway, and had a sense of the strange omission.

"Hello, dad!" she said, banging into the dull kitchen and startling a man sitting over accounts. He put them away with almost a look of fear. Jonathan Peel was a little man, with thin grey hair, and an apologetic look on his face.

"Why, lass," he said, and took her by the shoulder. His face brightened as she looked back at him. He was thinking that this one successful investment of his life was good to look at. He was also thinking that they must go on, that they couldn't spoil the girl's chance.

"Where's mother?" she asked.

"Bakehouse!" he answered.

She dashed off.

Mrs. Peel was standing at a long table, its top covered with tiny tarts, just filled with jam.

"Goodness, mother!" was the shocked exclamation of the girl. "Have you been ill?"

Mrs. Peel smiled. The smile spread ineffable sweetness over her tired face.

"Nothing to mention," she said cheerfully, and got the tarts in. Miriam sat on a backless chair whilst they baked, watching her mother. The keenest student of Shakespeare in Professor Merton's class was bringing her psychological insight to bear on the drama going on in her home.

"Who are the people over the way?" she asked.

"Oh — Smith's," said her mother. "They started six months since. I forgot to mention it. They don't do much. Then she found the tarts needed seeing to.

That night, after supper, Miriam made her parents go out for a walk — told them she'd come through the park, and wanted them to see the river swallows — and she would serve in the shop. They did not resist. When they had gone she got out the account books her father had put by with a good attempt at carelessness. Half an hour's study of them brought forth a long whistle.

Just then the door bell rang. She darted into the shop.

"Any 'Black Cat'?" asked a nice young man, with a dreamy look in his eyes.

Miriam was yet mixed in those mixed accounts.

" We don't stock cats," she observed hazily, "but — we might get some by tomorrow!"

Then she caught his eye. It was a brown eye—that gleamed suddenly. They looked at one another for a ludicrous moment, then burst out laughing.

"I was thinking of something else," said Miriam. " I had forgotten all about cigarettes."

She served him, and as he went off she could not refrain watching him through the window, when, to her horror, he entered the shop across — the shop of their rivals, the people who she said bitterly were killing her mother and making her father grey. He was patronising folk like those. She waited to see him come out. He did not come. He did not come out because he lived there!

When her parents came in she was sitting in the kitchen, frowning at 'King Lear'—on the lamplit table.

"See the swallows?" she asked, over supper. "Oh, but you should see them in the sunlight, the dark blue and the white."

Then she went to bed with a great ache in her young heart, to think of the gloom that had come on the two tired faces from that glimpse of the river, fading away under the old struggle.

When next she met the young man who had asked for Black Cats she gave him a proud and austere look.

"Girl across has red hair — awful colour," said the young man's sister. "I wonder how long they'll stick it yet? I've heard the old chap has overdrawn his account at the bank. Freddie was taking the money in for the firm when the clerk was mentioning it."

Meanwhile Mrs. Peel visibly worsened.

From her dip into the old romances, the Shakespearean scholar began to judge her father.

She grew desperate for fear of her mother.

"Dad," she said one day, openly facing the little gray man. "You're killing mother. Nothing justifies that. Nothing. There's no wealth but life. Ruskin said that. But if 'Comic Cuts' had said it, it would be just as true. Look here. I'll not have a career built on mother's broken body."

They stood and faced each other, whilst from the bakehouse came Mrs. Peel's cheerful, tired voice, singing 'Weary gleaners'.

The face of the little man grew sharp and thin. "I shall drive the other chap out," he said. "He's goin', then we can afford a baker. There's creditors."

"If you kill my mother I'll be your biggest," said Miriam, suddenly white. Dad Peel shrunk back from the young face.

They did not see the girl that night. She sat up in the big room upstairs, "studying" so she said.

The next evening she went to the masked ball at Narrowfield, and it came to pass she danced with the young man at the corner shop, and, not knowing him. found him interesting.

"You!" she said when they unmasked.

"Me!" he said ungrammatically for a chartered accountant.

It was raining when they reached the door to leave. He hired a cab. And somehow or other the whole story of the struggle across came out — rather closely. And, being a dreamy, forgetful young man he went off with a pair of satin slippers in his coat pockets.

He had a great scheme, and told Miriam of it by the river. He had almost written a short story, and would send it in to a competition, the prize being one hundred pounds. On condition that Mr. Peel took a milk business back in the country (one was advertised in Miriam's mother's old county) he would give Mr. Peel the money. Lend it, corrected Miriam. Of course he would win. That was all settled. Miriam read the story.'

Meanwhile down came inspectors of lard on Mr. Peel. And down came a the summons. Mr. Peel had no guarantee his lard was lard, though he paid the price. It would be fifty pounds.

"Have to get out now," said the young man's sister.

He gave her a fierce look and went off to look at the river swallows. He and Miriam sat on a little bench by a scented Daphne bush.

"If you win," she said, with a strange look, "don't come to the rescue right away. I want to see dad lose the world — for mother. Don't check the issue. I want to see it. If love isn't that — when one's getting on, and not — blooming — it isn't worth the candle."

She went off, and left him sitting in the dusk, with the sweet, sad scent of the Daphne bush in his soul.

****

Mrs. Peel had not baked this morning. She was too ill, and lay in bed.

Downstairs she could hear the little shop sounds. When the papers came she trembled violently — got up and dressed herself. She came down and found Mr. Peel and Miriam in the kitchen, Miriam reading the paper. She did not dare to ask for it. The girl's face looked wan in the morning light.

"How this morning?" asked Peel. His voice was jerky, his face pale. He moved indecisively and got his wife a chair.

Miriam did not move. She was reading.

The young man had not won in the great competition. He could interfere with destiny. She was reading a story written by a woman.

"I have decided," said Peel, suddenly.

His hand clutched his wife's chair back.

Miriam lifted her eyes.

"I have decided," said Peel, "to leave this damned hole, wife. I've got work in a shop, and can pay off the fine. We'll go in the country."

Thus went pride, the old dream of a shop of his own — everything.

Miriam flung down the paper without looking to see the name of the lucky competitor.

Her mother's face was a study. It was like a girl's.

Then, absently, the tired woman took up the paper Miriam had flung down, looking at it as to hide her tears. She had not thought Jonathan thought so much of her.

Her face changed again.

"Look!" She said, and pointed to a paragraph. "Look! You could win yet, Jonathan! Stay and bait then!"

Looking, Miriam saw that the lucky winner was — her own tired mother!

"I've made up my mind at last," said Peel. "We'll buy a milk business and live in the country."

They did.

Mrs. Peel, like many another competition winner, never tried again. She had tried to save her husband's dream. With him the miracle had happened.

Miriam must have thought the game of love worth the candle after all. The family across have ceased to refer to her as having red hair, but say her brother's young lady is 'auburn'. And no longer in that corner shop hangs out the offensively large card, with a black hand pointing across at the other shop saying, 'We defy competition'.

Cotton Factory Times, July 5, 1918

Jerry's courtship; the handicap

Jerry Dawson sauntered slowly up the village green, passing Giles' Smithy twice. And each time he passed it he was conscious of his rival's glorious six feet one inch of physical manhood.

He could have put up with the six feet. It was the one inch that worried him, because that one inch made people say of Adam Giles, "over six feet in his stockings," which caused Jerry to wish he stood in his shoes. Moreover, he felt that if he had been fed on good beef and bread, as Adam had, in his childhood, instead of margarine and treacle, he might not have been so skimpy.

He knew he hadn't a ghost of a chance, yet he couldn't keep away from the house at the end of the village — the house with the muskpots in the parlour window, and the prettiest girl in the place looking over them.

This time he met her — shopping. He suggested that he carried the basket for her. She allowed him to do it, much as she would allow a pet talk to carry the same article in its mouth.

"Going to Cherrydale tomorrow?" Asked Jerry, in what he meant to be a bold voice.

She looked out of her eye-corner's into the smithy as she answered — seeing the god-like form of Adam, swinging the iron down on the anvil, and making the sparks fly out.

"H'm! Yes! You goin', Jerry?" She asked, satisfaction that Adam had seen her walking with Jerry, in her voice.

"I'm goin'," said Jerry with a boldness that turned his face pale.

"All Daisy Thorpe's goin' " said Mitty.

"I'm going with you," quoth Jerry.

It was his nearest approach to open courtship. His heart was a sledge-hammer now in his stunted body. For whatever else was stunted Jerry's heart was not. He had decided on a school-bench, long ago, that he would marry Mitty.

"There'll be almost a round dozen of us," said Mitty.

And there was. There was a baker's dozen — thirteen — and, crossing the field paths to Cherrydale, the conversation turned on the old superstition.

The last field before they came out on the road to town showed a warning notice:-"Beware of the bull".

"Oh!" screamed Mitty.

"Frightened?" queried the big blacksmith. "Why, I could choked him with my fist."

She looked up at him.

Again Jerry cursed his meagre upbringing. He resolved determinedly that if he had ever any children he'd put blood in them via beef and good bread, and gallons of milk. They should never be at this disadvantage. He looked at his own shadow crossing the field.

Adam was helping Mitty over the stile.

The bull looked mildly at the party as they went. Jenny was wont to tell afterwards that he was sure it winked at him.

The five rival melodies of the five rival roundabouts came to them, and grew ever louder. It was the best fair Cherrydale had had for years.

They walked through an alley of brandy-snap stalls, and were into the din of the fair, jostling in and out the crowds — a laughing, jesting, pushing, half child-like crowd.

After Adam had swung the great hammer, and got his penny back for bringing out the old man at the top of the blow-register, Mitty hung on to his arm.

"You're gotten a grand lad!" said an old country woman, her bonnet aslant and a tickler in her hand, with which she tickled Adam's chin as she went past.

Mitty blushed under her dainty hat.

"Am I thy lad, Mitty?"

Jerry, at their heels like an un-noticed, un-wanted, but determined dog, heard the question.

But what Mitty said was drowned by the blair of a trumpet blown by a clown who had the paradoxically sad look of all clowns.

"Come up! Come up! Come up! This way for the wonder — "

And then Mitty heard the roaring of lions, and saw a swarthy man with skins over his shoulder.

"Tyrant — the man-devouring lion! South African lion, who has eaten four keepers. Twopence to see the brave Liosto enter the cage and whip him!"

Mitty's eye grew large with a look of worship. "Oh, I do love brave men," she said.

"I have heard," piped Jerry, as they walked up the steps, "that people always admire virtues they haven't got."

Mitty flashed an angry look. And Jerry realised that Adam had actually dared to support Mitty up the wooden steps. Clearly out of the running!

Bread and treacle! Might as well have put him out to die, as the ancient Greeks put out their weaklings.

He hummed a funny, tuneless tune as he went after Mitty and Adam, passing the cages. But he made comment on the monkeys, and the wild-cat, apparently talking to Mitty. But she saw no one but Adam. Then they gathered round to see the counting elephant.

The terror, the thrill, the wonder of the girls! They all fell in love with the man who entered Tyrant's cage, and enraged him, and made him roar till the place shook, and then leapt out just in time to avoid the giant form — the wide jaw full of awful teeth.

"I could do it myself," quoth Adam. "It's all a put up job."

And Jerry saw by the light in Mitty's eyes that the little idiot believed him.

But he managed once to get Mitty all by herself in a razzle-dazzle that hurled them round so they could see nothing but the blue and red painted organ in the centre of the roundabouts, and lightning flashes of little bronze images playing mechanical bugles, and a giddy swaying crowd below the roundabout, and lights — lights beginning to tumble from cocoa-nut stalls and shooting galleries.

"Mitty," yelled Jerry, looking sick, either from the motion of the roundabout or from fear, "I love you! Will you marry me?"

Then he lowered his hold on the back of the seat, and was pitched 'gainst her. He seized her waist imploringly.

"Jerry Dawson! Take your arm away. I couldn't marry a little man," said the indignant beauty.

Bread and treacle! Curse bread and treacle! Then something flared out in him.

"No, but you could flirt with one!" he said. By the feeling of her pretty face he saw that she had heard even above the din. When she got out she paid for her own ride, and ran to Adam as if for protection. Jerry found himself on his own madly bringing cocoa-nuts down, till a crowd gathered round.

"Look at the little chap. Hits 'em every time!" quoth somebody.

Jerry let the balls fall from his hands without trying anymore. You little chap. Oh, lord, that bread and treacle. He walked off without turning his head, and ignoring the crowd yelling at him to take the cocoa-nuts he had won.

"Want to go on the horses?" He asked an under-size, smudgy-cheeked child.

Big eyes grew bigger. "Fed on bread and treacle, I suppose?" said Jerry to the child.

Then he saw that Adam and Mitty were behind him on one horse. The child talked to him until the speed got up, then screamed, and Jerry soothed the frightened heart. As he got down, a woman seized hold of the child.

"Not lost! Been with big man on gee-gee!" said the youngster.

It was late that night when the party gathered itself together, and set out homewards. Gradually the lads and lasses paired off. Adam took Mitty. Jerry was the odd one. He walked with his hands in his pockets, humming the tuneless tune. Then he started — in the dimness of the moonlight he had seen Adam's dark sleeve about Mitty's waist. He shut his eyes in agony, screwing them up.

Then a terrified scream cut the air. He opened them to see the party scattering.

"The bull! The bull! Jerry — look out!" It was Mitty's voice.

The stile was near but the huge, infuriated figure of the bull loomed darkly as it came on with lowered head and lashing tail.

They were tumbling over the stile.

And —

Quite suddenly it was borne in on Jerry that the stalwart blacksmith, the man who had boasted he could tame a lion himself, was over on the other side of the stile, and Mitty on his side.

"Run, Mitty, run," he shouted at her.

She mechanically obeyed his voice. She was running in little, uneven steps, and the bull was gaining on her. Jerry saw that he must do something. His hand darted into his pocket. He danced towards the bull — weaving a gaudy ribboned rick rack, with its clicking sound startling the bull. The animal, after the pause that gave Mitty her chance, came towards Jerry. The battle between the blind rage of the animal and the far-seeing, cold-blooded rationalism of the human being began. Jerry backed and dodged, and hurled himself sideways, whilst an audience on the other side of the stile wondered that Jerry Dawson should have in him so much of the hero and the acrobat.

Once it seemed that Gerry must be tossed up on these cruel horns.

But when Mitty dared look again he was still there, a valiant figure. The bull's movements were not so certain now; they were flagging. But with a last desperate spirit of rage the animal plunged forward with a roar like the tone of a great bell.

Jerry stepped aside.

The bull missed him by half a yard and crashed into the hedge.

Jerry was over the stile.

The next moment he was the centre of the crowd. Girls adored him.

"It was nothing," he said modestly. "I'm such a little chap, you see. It has its advantages."

"You're a great big man," said Mitty's voice, quietly. "I didn't tell you, girls, that Jerry asked me to marry him a bit since, and I said 'yes'."

Later she told Jenny that she had liked him along — really — only it needs a little courage to walk out with a little man, unless you absolutely know — he's a great big man — really.

Cotton Factory Times, September 13, 1918

Old Tom's Christmas box; the penny goose

Old Tom sat in the doss-house, trying to get warm. The fire was big enough, it is true. But he didn't seem to have much success in sending the shivers away. The doss-house lamp just served to show up the discomfort of the place. Big Charley was trying to play 'Hail Smiling Morn' on his clarionette, but the very clarionette sounded drunk, and Big Charley always played erratically when in this state. Some of the tramps were in bed. Some were out at the 'Fanny Brown'.

"What's up wi' thee, Tum?" quoth Deputy Duckworth, who was cleaning up the fireside, in a huge apron, and in a man's clumsy way that bothered old Tom.

"Thee get on wi' thy mollying about," said old Tom.

Christmas always did bother old Tom. As he sat staring into the fire he saw a long line of Christmases, good, bad and indifferent, flit before his mind's eye. There could not be so many more. So how be it, he thought, and, getting up, he put on his overcoat and went out into the snowy streets. Snow! There seemed no end of it. It was underfoot, twelve inches deep, on the roofs, and the grey sky seemed to hold an invisible feather bolster that went on fluttering white feathers down without end.

People were shopping.

Whenever he saw a fat middle-aged woman just plodding along with a casket, he thought of Sarah. She would be shopping for Christmas. And he—whom she had taken for better, for worse, would have no Christmas dinner, unless he reckoned that big onion with salt and dry bread in his doss-house cupboard. It had been all worse he knew. But, had he had a goose, and she only a Spanish onion, he would have gone half with her.

Head down, he plodded along through the snow.

He had a way of walking with his head down. Maybe, it was the head following the inclination of his heart. It happened, therefore, that he did not see a red-faced man across the street looking at him as if about to come across, then walk on.

He stopped to read a bill advertising the 'Messiah'. He read the old names over. 'He Was Despised,' 'Hallelujah Chorus'.

Then he plodded on through the snow.

The picture of Sarah's comfort this Christmas embittered him. He could see it all. All the pictures would be decked with holly and mistletoe, and the clock—and on the shelves of the cupboard the fat brown jars that held mincemeat. The children would come home to their Christmas dinner, bringing their children.

Neddy Greaves would carry Christmas in, Sarah answering, watching him lest he dropped the cob of coal and her luck with it. Luck! He felt round and round his pockets. There was nothing but a bachelor's button, a broken stemmed pipe, and a pawn ticket for the only pair of shoes that did not let in the water. And it was all his own fault. That, also, was another piece of bitterness. There were men who could blame their own misery on other people. Old Tom had had an honest old Calvinist for a mother, a mother whose god was Oliver Cromwell, hater of shams.

"Tha looks down in the mouth, old cock." said a genial voice.

Tom stared into the face of Ebenezer George, likewise wifeless and homeless, but gaily careless of it.

Ebenezer jingled the money in his pocket.

"Conic and wet thy whistle," he said, and they went through the snow to the 'Fanny Brown'. They were very merry whilst the snow came down, and the ale went down, and Ebenezer kept saying "Go on, Tom".

Then, when spent up, they rose and went out into a night of cold stars, cold snow, and cold Christianity that looked at them soberly and said 'Drunk'.

Ebenezer said he was going home to spend Christmas and asked Tom to go with him. But a five mile tramp to a door that would not open did not appeal to Tom. He had been with Ebenezer before. Ebenezer's wife had a separation order, and could and would get the police.

So, Ebenezer went alone.

Old Tom went back to the doss house.

In order to pay his doss he had to get back the fivepence he had expended on his cupboard key, and pretend to be leaving. He was only out an hour, and came back, and paid his doss, but had to go without cupboard key. What was the good of a cupboard key anyhow, when all he had to steal was a Spanish onion and half a loaf? To make quite sure he got those, he ate them—tears in his eyes, either from grief, or the onion, or both. He had just one penny left. He went off to bed—into that bleak, long room with a line of beds, each holding a tramp.

Joe Bluff stumbled past him an hour later, waking him with his shouting.

"Anybody want to buy a raffle ticket?" he shouted. "I'll sell it for a penny."

"Here," said Tom, and handed him the penny which he had placed under his pillow.

Joe gave him the ticket.

When he got up in the morning Tom had forgotten all about the ticket until he saw it. A foodless day loomed before him. He knew the ticket would be worthless. He never won anything except full measure of punishment for his shortcomings. He had what he called facetiously "wind-pudding " to his breakfast, meaning nothing.

"Tha can have a chop wi' me," said the clarionette player, now dead sober.

There was a great bustle in the doss-house before dinner. At eleven o'clock the place held varied smells, varying from that of kippers and potatoes to real duck and Yorkshire ducks.

"By th' man!" ejaculated the clarionette player, looking at a man who had entered, holding a fat goose by its yellow feet.

"Somebody's goin' to have a good do," said the man, grinning.

Then he said, "Where's Joe Bluff?"

Joe Bluff came down to breakfast at this moment.

"This is thine, Joe," said the man.

"It is —hello!" shouted old Tom, jumping out of his chair.

Joe laughed.

"I sold him my ticket." he said, calmly.

Old Tom could scarcely lift the goose.

"Th' oven's full up," said the deputy. "Tha'll have to have 't to thi tay, Tom."

"I'll see about that," said Tom.

He walked out of the doss-house with the goose, attracting no small attention as he walked along. Wasn't there an oven in a Christian land to cook a poor old tramp weaver's goose on a Christmas morning?

He didn't believe it. He walked along, looking at various little windows, various little doors, until he came to a house where he thought he had a chance. He knocked on the door, which wanted paint, and from which a number had tumbled off. He had gone to the poorest house in a poor street.

A thin, worried looking young woman came to the door.

"Merry Christmas, said Tom. "Could you cook me this, missis?"

He held up the goose. She eyed it enviously. She had grey eyes, and would have been pretty but for that excessive thinness and the look of worry.

"You can have half of it for the cooking," said Tom.

Her eyes lit up. She pushed three small children, who had come to see what was going on, back into an untidy house. Upon a settle in the kitchen was stretched her husband asleep—and drunk.

Tom had that irritation at the sight, only explained by the fact that he was sober, and it was the morning after.

He sat on a chair at the back of the house, and began to pull feathers off the goose, but she made him come up to the fire. Some rosy colour had stolen into her cheeks at the sight of some dinner for herself and the children, and, perhaps, also for him, a fool that he was.

"It's the blind leading the blind, lass, I think," said old Tom. "Well, we neither of us could ha' done without t' other. Tha's getten an oven—an' I've getten a goose."

The children began to play with the feathers flying round the old man's chair. They somehow reminded Old Tom of his own children, who he scarcely realised would be as old as they were. He had never seen either Sarah or them for over twenty years. He had not the moral courage of some of the tramps.

"My mother's coming, you see," said the young woman. "That's what bothered me. She doesn't know he's as bad as he is." She jerked her head in the direction of the man on the settle. "If he could nobbut sleep it off afore she lands," she said, wistfully.

Then she started in to sweep up the kitchen, take up cinders, whiten the hearth, and scour the fender. It seemed as though sights of the goose had given her new courage to face life.

"I were wondering what on earth I'd tell her," she confessed to Tom, alluding to her mother. "I'd naught but some spuds and a bit o' fat in the house, and two loaves. But she'll wonder who you are."

"Oh, I'll explain myself," said Tom. "By! but this is a rare goose! Worth a penny, so how be it!" which made the young woman laugh, seeing which the children laughed, and the house grew lighter, somehow.

By one o'clock the goose was almost ready. It was beginning to "kick up a smell," and the potatoes were beginning to boil in a pan over the bright fire. The children had clean faces, clean pinnies, and their hair combed, and Annie—who had lent her oven for half the goose—was washed, and had put on her least shabby blouse, and tried to put her hair up in the style.

"I'd a lass called Annie," said Old Tom. "Funny, isn't it?"

The remarkable coincidence in a world full of Annie's made them both smile.

The young woman stitched his sleeve into decency. He washed himself, brushed his hair, straightened his tie, and was riding the youngest child on his clumsy Blucher shoe, when a knock came.

"My mother!" said Annie.

She came in —an old woman, with white hair, a much-lined face, and a way of walking that said she knew what

127

was what. But Old Tom know her. It was Sarah—Sarah, who bore the marks of poverty —withal respectable poverty —and disappointment. Sarah, who had no home to deck with holly; Sarah, who was housekeeping, and had a hard shop of it. too. They were introduced. She didn't know him. She was too tired, too disinterested in life to look closely at strangers, she who had dropped in to Christmas dinner.

"Jack ill?" she asked, taking off her bonnet and nodding at her son-in-law.

"Not so weel," said Annie, and gave her the cloth to spread.

"We'll let him have his sleep out," she said as they sat down without Jack.

Oh, what a meal it was! Old Tom could scarcely see clear. To think of Sarah without home. Oh, what an old fool he had been. Then he was carving the goose. What a goose!

"If thi father'd done what he should," said Annie's mother, suddenly, "we could have had a goose like that every Kestmas. Whereas both him and me's knocked about like workhouse spoons. I wonder where he is? You get thinking that way —once a year."

"Ay, ay," said old Tom.

Why, her hair was quite white. It bothered her somehow. Some of that white he'd woven into the black, he knew.

"What did they call your husband, missus?" he asked, looking across the table at her, whilst Annie gave the kiddies "more, more—"

She told him.

"I know him," he said.

She gasped—whitened. "What's he like? she asked.

"Summat like me," said Old Tom.

She studied him bald, ill-clad. "To think," she observed to Annie, "'at thy father should be aught like that!"

"If you like, I'll take you to see him," said Old Tom.

" Nay," she said.

But after dinner she observed she wouldn't mind seeing him, seeing it was Christmas, and it weren't far away. To think of Sarah caring in so much!

Old Tom waited for her to get ready. Then he took her towards the doss-house. He took her into the bare room with the little cupboards, the big fire, and the benches. Deputy was asleep in his chair.

"To think Annie's father lives here," she said. Then, "Where is he?"

"Stop there, an' I'll fetch him," said Old Tom.

Ho had half a mind to go out and never come back. But ho went out, and came in again.

"Couldn't ta find him?" asked Sarah.

"Yigh," said Old Tom. "He's here."

He seized himself by the buttonhole. She stared at him a long time.

"Well," she said at length, tha'rt a sample, anyway."

But after a little talk they decided to spend the day at Annie's. When they got back Jack was awake, and quite sober, washed, eating his dinner. He had made another Christmas resolution, and he kept that one. The thought of getting to be like Annie's father was too much for him.

Old Tom went back to the doss-house, not quite forlorn. He had had a merry Christmas, a warm Christmas, and— hope springs eternal in the human breast. Maybe, he thought, that Christmas box would lead to him and Sarah having a home of their own yet, and decked with holly, just as he had dreamed she would deck it.

Cotton Factory Times, December 20, 1918

Tom Bobbin's revenge; the stolen pie

Tom Bobbin was one of those men whose chief topic of conversation is—grub. His mother said it all came from his being born in the Cotton Panic, when she had been forced to think a lot about what he didn't get. Be that as it may, Tom was a belly god and made no bones about the fact. But there were a lot of things he bore quietly that lots of men would have said they couldn't bear at all. With a wife that nagged, a bonnie little lass born blind, and an everlasting struggle to make his six looms keep his family of four children, Matty, and himself, Tom needed all the comfort he could out of a good potato pie or a beef pudding.

Round-ended, twinkle-eyed, Rosie, rosy-faced, Tom worked at his six looms very contentedly. Friday he always whistled a lot, for Friday brought a steak-pudding at dinner, and wages at night, and he always treated himself to an odd pint of beer on the way home — no more — for he was fonder of his children, and said that they shouldn't start life on poor grub if he could help it.

Now, next to Tom worked a long, lean man the weavers had nick-named Ba-Lamb, because he cured sheepskins for a hobby. He lived with his old mother, and had never been wed, and said he never would.

This chap got sick and weary of hearing Tom bragging about Matty's steak-pudding, or else he was a bit envious, for his mother had ill-health and couldn't stand the smell of cooking. Be that as it may he decided to play a trick on Tom, and told all the weavers round about him what he meant to do. That is, the men weavers. They felt it wasn't safe to trust women, for Tom was a favourite with all the women.

One rainy Friday dinner-time, just as the picking sticks began to move slower, and the engines to slacken, like a heart that was running down, Tom went down into the engine-house, as usual, for his dinner.

"Tha's had none brought to-day, Bobbin," said the engine tenter.

Tom stared until old Daniel thought his eyes were coming out of his head.

"Here, what arta givin' us?" said Tom.

After a lot of arguing, Tom found out that little Bob had not brought his dinner into the engine-house that day. But the watch-house woman said she had opened the door for him with her own hands at twenty past twelve. Somebody must have way-laid him on his way across the yard.

Tom was in a fix. He just twopence in his pocket. His home was two miles away. And — as he stood in the mill-yard, the rain trickling down his collar, his face as glum as a tombstone — he saw long Bill, and several other chaps, go past him grinning. He remembered how he bragged of Matty's puddings, and also that Bill had said she'd be forgetting to send it one of these days.

Tom was a chap that didn't show all in his face that moved in his heart. Not that he was deceitful, either. But as he moved slowly across the yard, out through the gates, and towards a cook-shop, he felt he would like to murder somebody. He pondered how to get his own back, as he gloomily surveyed the stars of grease on the top of his twopenny worth of 'broth'. But he had no ideas.

After dinner, when he got back to his looms, he found the empty pudding dish, with a scrap of paper inside, on which were written these words:

"If any man has aught that's good,
Let him give thanks and say no mour;
Or wish until it's safe inside,
For in this world there's nought that's sure."

He also found another scrap of paper like it inside Long Bill's weft tin. So he was sure he was on the right man.

When he got home that night he told Matty, and after she'd called him every name she could find, for fool, she agreed with him that they couldn't pass this over.

The weavers round about thought Tom a very tame man not to kick up a bother about that pudding.

Bill was a bit sorry they had eaten it, particularly when Tom invited him to his Sunday tea.

What a tea that was which Matty made. It cost ten shillings. But revenge, like other things, can't be had at naught.

Bill was surprised to see what a fine home Tom had out of just one wage. He didn't know the tablecloth was borrowed, likewise the spoons, and that the whole family was decked out in hired clothes. He began to think that some day he wouldn't have his mother to potter after him, and had best lookout for a wife as good as Matty. Little Nettie, the blind lass, sat on his knee, and perhaps it was her bonny little face made him have hard work to keep from conferring about the steak-pudding. But only the thoughts of the fool he'd look held him back.

That night Matty's youngest sister came in after chapel. She was as bright as a button and as bonnie as wax, and when Bill had tasted a pie Tom assured him she had made, the thing was done.

But it took four more tea drinkings to bring the climax.

After the last Bill wrote and asked Sarah if she'd meet him on Monday at seven o'clock by a thorn-bush by a little bridge between her home and his. She wrote back that she'd be pleased to meet him at 8 30 if he didn't mind.

So it was on the edge of dusk when Bill, dressed up, and feeling like he'd St. Vitus Dance, went towards that bonnie pink thorn tree.

She was then alright. She looked tall to him, somehow, but he thought it was his focus had got wrong. His heart was going like a sledge-hammer and he didn't look at her much. She'd a veil on, too. How she trembled when she took his arm.

When they had walked a mile or two they sat down on a form near a little wood, when birds were twittering good-neet to one another.

Then, feeling he couldn't go on like this any longer, Bill said:

"Sarah, does ta love me?"

Sarah said nothing.

"Don't be flerried o' sayin' if tha' does," said Bill.

He slipped his arm round her waist.

She trembled again.

"Give us a kiss," said Bill.

But quite half-an-hour went past before she'd agree, and by this time it was almost dark and everything was quiet save for a corncrake making his racket in the wet grass. Bill had confessed all sorts of things to Sarah, gone on his knees to her, and made a right fool of himself. An now, at last, she promised to kiss him. He hardly knew if the stars were staying over his head, or if he sat on them, as he leaned forward. She had lifted up her veil.

The next moment he felt a man's moustache brush his face, gave a wild shout that scared the corncrake, and may it miss a beat, and took to his heels like old Nick. While a chap's laughter rang out after him. It wasn't Sarah. He had made love to her cousin Bob.

When he got home and put his hand in his pocket to draw out a handkerchief to mop his forehead he also pulled out a scrap of paper. On it were written these words:

"Let no man steal another's meat,
Puddings nor pies, with knavish trick,
And think he's got off with a treat,
For such are not fit to be wick.
    Or if he does, let him give thanks
    He's got off without broken Shanks."

Poor Bill! He knew by the time he got working that the tale was all through the weaving-shop, and all the women said it served him right. All but Sarah! After all they made it up, and were married before the Wakes. But he had a sad disillusionment when he tackled her first pie, and found out that Tom's revenge was not quite over. She had never made a pie in her life before. When he had her first temper he was further astonished. When she had turns he had ceased to be astonished at anything, and, being a right man after all, he set out to sell hot peas in a little barrow, in addition to curing ba-lamb skins and weaving in the day time.

As for Matty, she showed Sarah how to make right beef-puddings, and Bill said, in a burst of confidence to Tom, once, that after all, there were compensations in life.

Cotton Factory Times, February 28, 1919

"Engaged": the frump

There was something exhilarating in the pantomime that night. The principal boy was bewitching, and Cinderella danced like a fairy. The comedian was one of the first water. And the three young men who came out arm in arm were notable practical jokers. Tom Burns, the tall one, had often got himself into holes by his jokes.

It was just as they reached the rainy street, reflecting the street lamps, that he unveiled to the eyes of his companions a board brought from the theatre. Upon it, in great, staring, black letters, were the words:-

"ENGAGED"

Before they recovered their breath Tom had hurried them along, spying in the crowd three women, also walking arm in arm. Their back views were not entrancing. They were obviously back numbers, having reached the bunion and out-of-date jacket stage. The one in the middle was possibly the youngest. There was a certain air of vitality in her movements, and it was possible she was suiting her pace to that of her older companions. But she was a frump. Her dress reached her boots. She had not given way to that resolution in legs which unmistakably divides the old from the rising generation.

As the light from a shop window fell on her back Tom saw two big, brown buttons. It was the work of a moment to hang the string of the theatre board upon these two buttons. The joke commenced.

Utterly unconscious of the sensation she was creating, the woman cautiously piloted her two companions over the street.

Behind them followed a small, laughing crowd, careful not laugh too loudly. A few people said it was a shame.

"Oh, they're goin' into a shop!" said Tom.

"Come on," said Fred Brooks.

They followed into the tea-room, The waitress tried not to smile as she read the board. It was when the young woman tried to sit down that she discovered the joke.

For she was young, and not uncomely. She blushed to the roots of her brown hair, and tears of mortification sprang into her eyes. Then she did a thing that made the three young men stare.

She took a piece of brown paper from her bag, and parcelled up the board.

She took tea, and got it for her two companions very quietly. They were loud in their exclamations against the 'commonness' of this generation. They were illiterate and trenchant. Tom set them down as 'charwomen' who would like a glass of supper stout. The young woman was harder to reckon up. Her dress was frumpish. But there was a curious refinement in the way she took that cup of tea. And the three young men had the uncomfortable feeling that she suspected them.

The joke had somehow fallen flat.

As he paid at the pay-box, Tom Burns saw her eyes. Then and there he fell in love with those eyes. He passed out into the street, with his friends, calling himself a callous ass. He had hung the theatre board on the back of a girl with eyes like those. But —oh —her clothes!

Some weeks passed.

He still felt the influence of the eyes of the unknown woman who was a frump, yet no frump.

To get their beauty out of his mind, he accepted an invitation to his father's old friend. Whilst there he attended a dance. It was as he was leading the daughter of his father's old friend through the dance set down on the country programme as 'Tickle Toes', that he saw the Eyes again.

But, oh, the transformation! They looked dreamily out over a dress that could only be written as a 'creation'.

"Who is she?" asked Tom, of his partner.

"Marjory Bates. Her father's very rich. They both do odd things. She takes their charwomen to the theatre, and dresses like them, so as to make them feel at home. Awful things they do."

"Good lord!" said Tom.

"I'll introduce you," said Lilian.

She did. The girl of the Eyes looked at him. But she said her programme was full when he asked her for a dance.

Tom could not tell whether or not she recognised him as the one she suspected in the tea shop.

There was another dance later. She promised to sit one out with him.

As they went forwards they saw staring them in the face a board, on which was the awful word that made Tom redden: "ENGAGED." He pretended not to look at. it. They passed by the place sacred to the bandsmen—to the quiet room full of flowers.

And Tom did a most foolish thing. He proposed—on third sight—with the consciousness that his father had as much money as hers.

"I'm ENGAGED," she said, quietly, drawing her hand from his.

His dejection looked out of his eyes.

"For the next dance," she said.

Ho had to take her back, whilst he could not make up his mind whether or not she had specially chosen that word to let him know that she knew.

He wrote to her, afterwards, asking her to set him a time to make friends. The answer could not be a coincidence. It was merely: "Very busy. ENGAGED."

She knew! She had probably guessed it was he, himself.

He was in despair. "Is Miss—Bates engaged?" he asked the daughter of his host, later.

"She doesn't wear a ring," she said; "but she might be engaged by bracelet. It's modern not to wear rings."

Whereupon Tom thought of that old ring of his mother's which he would like to hand on only to the little hand he had first admired as he saw it lift a teacup to the prettiest mouth in the world, old clothes or not.

The next time he saw her she was fishing. He also was fishing. She was evidently out to catch trout, and caught them. She showed not the slightest consciousness that he had twice proposed to her.

They went to try and get tea at a little cottage, and were passing into a pleasant room with red ochred floor, when the lady of the house said "Excuse me. That room is engaged."

Tom looked up sharply, and thought he saw a smile on Marjory's lips.

On the way home he proposed again. Persistency was one of the Burns' family qualities.

"Please," said Marion, "say no more. I am engaged to be married to the most chivalrous man in the world."

And he knew she knew.

She knew that he was not chivalrous. He hung theatre boards on the backs of old frumps. But he did not know how all women, the frumpiest frumps, were now glorified because of her.

He met 'the most chivalrous man in the world' two weeks later. He might be chivalrous. But he had no hair worth a mention, and Tom wondered. She did not look quite happy with him. As for Tom, he went back to town, and put her out of his thoughts as well as he could.

****

It was six months later when he went to the house of his father's old friend again.

"How are the Bates's?" he asked Lilian, over the breakfast coffee.

She told him a wonderful tale. Old Bates was bankrupt. At the last moment the chivalrous man had given Marjory up, because he suspected she didn't 'fancy' him. Bates was dead. Marjory was a nursery governess at a village some miles away.

Tom Burns went to that village. He asked for, and was shown to where Miss Bates sat mending children's hose and telling fairy tales. And he proposed again.

"Excuse me," she said. "This is my employer's time. I'm ENGAGED."

Whereupon he confessed to the miserable business, and told how sorry he had been, what a cad he had felt, and how he wouldn't hang another board on another old frump, however he felt the impulse. And Marjory laughed.

He bought her a beautiful necklace. In return she sent to him a package, carefully tied with string and sealed. When he untied it, eagerly, behold the old theatre board, and upon the back was written "I've cared ever since I saw your laughing eyes in the tea shop!"

Cotton Factory Times, September 5, 1919

Miss Strange's Christmas; playing the part

At the end of the rutted lane leading from the lozenge-paned schoolhouse, Miss Strange saw the Merlin carriage waiting, as it had waited at this hour of each year, for her insignificant school-mistress self, for the past twenty years. Squire Merlin kept open house at Yule, and she was the educator of his tenantry.

Each year her invitation had brought the same pang, the same joy. To-night, she could not tell why, both were keener than usual. She set it down to the dream she had dreamt on the previous night, that disturbing dream wherein she had been young again, even whilst she had known it was only a dream, and had awakened with wet eyes, hearing again her mother's gentle voice, speaking those fateful words. "My dear, he could not mean it. Men in his station do not marry women in yours."

"A Happy Christmas, John," she greeted the old coachman, as she came up to the carriage.

"Same to you, and many of 'em," he responded heartily.

She remembered that he had thus responded twenty years. A little restless feeling, foreign to her quiet soul, passed over her as she stepped into the Merlin carriage, and the wheels crunched over the moonlit snow. Who knew? Had her mother been right, after all? But if she was wrong, why had he not kept his word? He had said, very gravely, on her third refusal, "I will ask you again in twenty years to prove to you that I have thought about it, that this is not just — folly."

How bitterly he had said that word —"folly."

For her attitude had wounded his pride. He had read the reflection of the village suspicion in her dignified refusal to consider his proposal other than as an infatuation. Twenty years ago!

When she reached Crow's Nest she handed her cloak to Will, the stiff-necked, silk-stockinged footman, with the feeling of humility he always inspired in her. Then she had a ludicrous sense of wonder as to how he would have fancied her as the mistress of Crow's Nest—supposing her mother, dead this past year, had been wrong. She passed him with a straighter back than usual.

In the great room, where her wedding feast might have been spread, they were dancing. She did not know the dances; they were not of her day, so she refused the offer of a young farmer to 'join in the fun'. She sat watching—a sweeter figure than she knew, in her black lace dress and the very successful artificial roses, in her hair, white enough to suggest powder beauties of old, though her face was yet fresh and placid.

"The barn dance," commanded handsome, lithe Winton Merlin. The fiddlers struck up the Roger de Coverley music at his bidding.

It was he, the nephew of another Winton Merlin, legal tenant of Crow's Nest, but long an absentee, who took Miss Strange's hand.

Looking at the youth, her dream seemed to be broken. She could almost imagine that the years had rolled back.

When he relinquished her hand she watched him cross over to a slight girl, with very yellow hair, and bend over her, a troubled devotion on his face that made it more like that other face she had not seen for years.

Eva Pritchard was 'rolling in money'—made out of toilet soap. Some of the wings at Crow's Nest were out of repair for lack of money. Winton Merlin could not speak; toilet soap lay between; and — Eva Pritchard was a woman, and, also, a Quakeress.

"Poor boy!" said Miss Strange to herself.

Half-an-hour afterwards the whole party, 'gentle and simple', turned out to hear the bells ring from Crow's Nest Walk.

Miss Strange, that odd feeling of restless in her again, followed out. She almost ran into the arms of a stout gentleman coming in a different direction.

Both apologised.

Miss Strange was proceeding after the others when the stranger held her back.

"Have you come from the Nest?"

"Yes," answered Miss Strange, a little surprised. Then she remembered that it was Christmas Eve.

"I'm in a beastly hole." said the gentleman. "I'm a—a friend of the Merlin's, and am bent on saving one of them from doing something disastrous to his welfare. It's Winton Merlin. He's almost drunk, and declaring he will propose to Miss Pritchard. If he does—she'll never listen to him again. He'll make a fool of himself before a crowd. No woman— she least of all—would marry a fool who proposed before a crowd. So I've fastened him up in the Clock Tower."

There was a little silence.

"What are we to do?" inquired the friend of the Merlin family.

"He must *not* do it," said Miss Strange, as no one but a schoolma'm could say it.

There was another silence.

Then, across the snow, from an ivy-mantled tower, that looked ghostly in the dim moonlight, came unghostly sentences — in an Oxford accent.

"Unless he is quietened, they will hear him," almost groaned the stout gentleman. "They will come back this way. I did not think of that. I had forgotten."

Then he said, impulsively, "You are just about her size."

"Eva Pritchard's?" inquired Miss Strange.

He surveyed the little figure that somehow seemed familiar to him.

Even as she wondered what he meant, he said: "If you could pretend to be Eva Pritchard, if you would go to him, listen to all his piffle for an hour—until this carriage has gone—I'd be eternally grateful."

"But I'm dark-haired," said Janet Strange.

"He's drunk," was the laconic answer. "And there's a blue wrap in the hall—like the one she wears. Oh, if you only knew what I care about the young idiot, how I want to save him from what I have suffered! Do help me!"

"I'll try," said Janet, bravely.

She went with the stranger into the hall.

"Janet!" he ejaculated, as the light shone on her.

141

She was old, yet—she was young, just as the dream had told her.

But she did not go back on her bargain.

She let him hold the ends of her little fingers for a moment and wished him a Merry Yule, with the restraint of a day that has gone.

Five minutes later, in the deceptive blue wrap, she ran across the snow to the Clock Tower.

"Eva'" came from within.

Janet realised that Young Winton was mad enough to think there was no one in the world but his yellow haired fascination, with her Quaker soul that would never overlook a public proposal.

She went up the worn steps. Winton's voice came to her, as she climbed by aid of a shaky rail.

She turned the key, entered—and something sprung at her, seizing her hand, falling on its knees, kissing the hem of her dress, pouring out its long pride-hidden affection.

"Oh, please don't!" protested poor Janet.

She felt a most barbarous hypocrite.

"It's been—the—hic—s—s—soap," he coughed. "And I must tell you, d-darling, Crow's Nest isn't mine. It's my uncle's. And he has come h-home to m-marry. I've n-nothing—but a-hic-Oxford accent, and—I'm a M-Merlin. You see, Eva, d-darling, I can't live on your father's money. Now can I? But I love you."

It was like the cry of her own youthful heart only —the cry in hers had always been feminine and sober.

Miss Strange was carried out of herself.

She knew, in some way, that if only she could play the part, she could knock down this barrier, this very material barrier of soap-money, making a barrier between two proud hearts.

"What does it matter," she murmured, "if we love each other, Winton?"

Which came as a so great a shock of happiness, to the 'young idiot' that he was sobered. She knew that he would remember in the morning and write to Eva Pritchard, and that Eva Pritchard —believing he had walked over his Merlin poverty pride would accept him, unable though she had been to encourage him, from sheer womanly pride.

He did not offer to kiss her, as the poor, school-ma'm had feared.

He stood up now. Only retaining her little hand, whilst Miss Strange was put through the half-tragic, half-humorous situation of answering such questions as "When did you first begin to love me —?"

She stuck to vague answers as safety.

The clock struck the half-hour.

Half an hour yet to fill in, before she was sure Miss Pritchard would be gone. To the end of her days she never would forget that interminable time that passed, until the bells rang out.

"A Happy Christmas, Eva darling," said young Winton.

Quite suddenly she realised that he was going to kiss her. Then, "I must go. They will miss me!" she said, frantically, and rushed out.

"Eva!" called Winton's voice. But the apparition in the blue wrap was gone.

He walked about ten minutes, to further sober himself, out in the snow and moonshine; and then went to the house, just before the merry party came past the old tower, Eva Pritchard with them. On the steps of the Nest Janet Strange trembled with anxiety lest anything should crop up between the two. But Pa Pritchard was present, and beyond helping her into the carriage, and looking at her with that shadow of pride lifted for ever from his young eyes, Winton Merlin said nothing.

"A Happy Christmas," said a pleasant voice.

He saw Janet Strange, the schoolmistress, waiting for the carriage to take her home. For the first time he noticed how like her voice was Eva Pritchard's.

"A Happy Christmas to you, also," he said, warmly.

Then he saw that his Uncle Winton had come out on the steps.

"I'll never forgive you, uncle," he said, recalling the indignity he had suffered of being locked in the Clock Tower.

"You'll thank me to the end of your days, you young fool," said his uncle, genially. Which, later, Winton agreed with.

As for Eva Pritchard, she answered "Yes," when that letter came, but thought for a moment that young Merlin's brain was turned from his references to her being with him in the Clock Tower. But when she met him in the great hall at the house built from soap, their first words were—a kiss, and though she was a little indignant at his supposing she would climb the Clock Tower in search of him, nothing mattered really, after that kiss.

Some months later the mystery of the woman who had answered in her name was made clear. Janet Strange was then Janet Merlin—and, as Winton said, it did not matter, seeing that it was now a family matter. For Janet Strange had believed the elder Winton that he had really "meant it. "—and it was not folly. Who wouldn't have done, after twenty years, and on Christmas Day too, with the carrollers singing, as he placed her into the old carriage.

Cotton Factory Times, December 26, 1919

John o' Bobs' last pint; the penitent's return

John o' Bobs (little John as his pals dubbed him, though he stood six foot one in his socks) groaned softly as he listened to Ann's vengeance for the way he had come home the night before.

"Eh, if tha'd only bin drunk — once!" said John o' Bobs, despairingly.

"Tha'd like to make ma as bad as thysel', but tha cannot," said Ann, whose tongue ran on again, clatter, clatter, until he began to believe that there was something in the picture she drew of him — that of an utter villain. Though, truth to tell, he was as soft as butter.

It was Friday morning. The engine had broken down at factory. Ann would be cleaning all day—between talking at him.

How to pass the long and weary hours he did not know. One thing was certain—he must escape temporarily from his wife. When she broke down and threatened to leave him if ever he came home in that state again, he reached the lowest depths in his hell of repentance. Moreover, what Ann was saying only clinched what he had been thinking when he had wakened at four that morning and couldn't sleep again because his tongue was like a nutmeg grater.

"Nay, dry up, lass!" he said, miserably. "I'll put an end to this. Just see if I don't."

"Till th' next time," sobbed Ann.

"Noa —I'll finish it off this time," said John, determinedly. "Na, I'll say nowt no moar. I've drunk my last pint. I'll go and get my face shaved."

So Ann dried her eyes, spread a newspaper on the kitchen table, set the fender thereon, and began to polish up its brasswork as if it were gold.

John went to hare his shave. Half-way down the old-fashioned street he met Billy Breeze.

"Shop's packed out," said Billy. "Come on an' have a — "

"Never again," said John. He had a martyr's look.

Billy looked puzzled.

"I'm joining the Temperance Club to-night," said John, unveiling his purpose to Billy, as he had not revealed it to Ann.

Billy did not laugh at him as John expected.

"Well, if a chap can't take a glass an' leave it, happen it's best," he said.

They talked on other matters for some time. Then Billy said musingly: "So we've had our last pint together, John!"

John suddenly felt that he was making great sacrifices for Ann. At the present moment his throat was like hot sand.

"Aye," he said, valiantly.

"Nay, just let's have a farewell drink—just to drink the health of the idea," said Billy.

The long years in which he would drink no beer loomed up before John's inner eye, "Our last one," he said valiantly, and they went into the Blue Heifer.

It was far on in the afternoon when they came out. Each man had upon his back a bundle containing food, a stick, and the company had gone round with the hat for them, and had wished them Godspeed.

They were going to America, walking it to Liverpool and going to work their passage out. On and on by the canal, whilst the dusk gathered, they walked. Billy leaned against a wall once, wept, and wanted to turn back to say good-bye to his wife, but John got him to go on. Then John wanted to go back, just to tell Ann how he would come home a millionaire, and Billy persuaded him not to do this, or they'd miss the boat.

They walked on until they were dog-tired, and America seemed further away than ever. Eventually they agreed that they had better have a little sleep. Finding an upturned fish-cart, the shafts in the air, they got into it, and slept. At the first glimmer of dawn they awoke. Birds were twittering. Frost was on the fields and over them. Their teeth chattered. They looked out on a sober, dull, and tragic world, very different from that they had surveyed only a few short hours ago, when they were going to conquer the globe.

As they warmed their noses over a pipe of tobacco they discussed the situation.

"I daren't face mine," said Billy.

It was well known that Billy's wife had once stitched him up in a sheet and thrashed him.

"Neither dare I face mine," said John. "I can't stan' a woman blitherin' — We'se ha' to go on, now."

At Brigden John remembered an old friend who lived there and went to seek him out. He tried to look glad to see them. He was newly married, living in a house approached by five white steps, and everything inside the house was new, from the scrubbing brush to the affection. George's wife looked at me two men in corduroys, and took the cushions off the chairs before asking than to sit down. But they had a good meal of eggs and bacon.

When George walked a hundred yards with them to put them on the way again, he said rawly: "What the Hanover did you come seekin' me out for? It'll take a month to explain this away! She's second cousin to a J.P., an' you look like a couple o' beggars."

Arm in arm Billy and John toddled off. "These women!" said John once.

"That's a true word," agreed Billy. "We've summat to do to suit them. But—they are faithful." Whereupon John got homesick again.

But, dropping into a pub, where a man was playing bagpipes, they gained a more hopeful outlook. John sang 'The Monarch of the Woods' in such voice that the company went round with the hat again, and the man with the pipes vowed lasting friendship with him. Some hours later he persuaded them to go home with him. They went, and tried to make themselves sober with strong tea. It was a house without house mother, and a crew of dishevelled children, who looked hatred at the pipes, whose music was often their only Sunday dinner.

"Have you aught on to-night, chaps?" asked the piper.

They looked glumly at each other.

They could go back and face their wives, or get on to Liverpool. The latter idea hurt the soles of their feet, and the former made them wince. They would have to face women who had been sitting up all night waiting.

They were drifting now.

"There's a go-as-you-please competition," said Sandy. "I'm trying. Happen I could get John in, too. I know the manager."

But John vowed nothing on earth would make him appear behind the footlights. However, after more beer, his mood changed. He had a dim recollection of being introduced to the manager, who apparently took his rough attire as part of his get-up, and he heard Sandy praising him up as the best bass singer in the county. He was told, too, that he was to appear, and sing 'Drinking'.

The rest was a mix-up, like a nightmare. He saw people strutting about, and waking roars of laughter from the pit, as through a cloud of smoke. There came a young man in evening dress, with a look that said he felt himself to be somebody. He sang 'Daddy', but the effect was lost as his collar was so high and there didn't seem much natural affection about him, but a lot of unnatural affectation, which said he considered he'd done them a favour to compete at all though the first prize was ten guineas.

Sandy went on. The pit rose to its feet. Sandy had a lot of friends. When he played 'Up wi' the Bonnets o' Bonnie Dundee' it looked as if there would be a fight.

Somehow or other John found himself staggering across the platform, dazed with the lights and conscious of a draught. He had a drunken sense that he had got to beat Sandy to win the prize, and that Sandy would take beating. He also remembered that it was 'Drinking' he had to sing, and far away at the back of his head was the picture of poor Ann, sitting up all night and waiting for him. A chair was put ready, and he staggered across to it—and silence fell.

"Rare fine actin'," said a northern voice.

But John was not acting. He sat down on the chair and sang 'Drinking', without the bucolic joy and with all the sober sorrow. But by the end of the second verse he had changed again. The lights were dancing before his eyes, and he felt ready for more beer, and Ann could wait for ever for all he cared. Whilst in the pit a pin could have been heard to drop.

"That chap's bin drunk, I'll bet," said the northern voice again.

"Put him out," said somebody, fiercely.

They wanted to listen to this stumbling, sorrowful, devil-may-care, thirsty, human voice, singing 'Drinking'. And as he sang the last verse John grew sleepy—drunkenly sleepy. The words came slowly and ever more slowly, His stare was like that of a man hypnotised. The last word dragged itself out—and he collapsed off the chair, whereupon the gallery went wild, and the pit rose up to meet the gallery, and the manager dropped the curtain, and had it wound up again, and finally said there was not time for an encore, whilst the pit shouted out for the voice of the new genius.

Other items came on at length. But John was prize winner. Sandy won second, and took him home, and Billy and all of them sat up—drinking again.

On a sunny Sabbath morning, with eight pounds in his pocket, John set back towards Ann, Billy with him.

"It's a' reight for thee," said Billy. "Tha can allus get a woman to forgie thee for summat 'at has paid. But —"

He turned his pockets out dolefully, whereupon John gave him two pounds.

"They're faithful creatures, said Billy. "Mare'll be waitin' yet—wi' th' rollin'-pin, She'll not ha' winked her eyes sin' I went."

They took the train, but half-way home decided it would be bad policy to go home on Sunday. The journey was finished on Monday morning —the first train. John asked Billy to see him home, and plead for him, and promised to do like service for him.

"For", said Billy. "a woman likes to hear other folk praisin' her husband, but she'll not believe his word at all."

They went through the quiet streets where the mill whistles had not yet screamed.

"Are th' blinds up, Billy?" asked John, dolefully, as they reached his street.

"They're drawn, like it were a deyd-house," said Billy.

John stared. It was true. Ann must have gone to bed after all.

They entered the house gently, without knocking, finding the latch yield. Voices floated out from the parlour.

"We've given orders for th' canal draggin'," said a man's voice. "But often they don't come up for a fortnight after."

Billy had much to do to hold John in hand, at this. For the voice was that of his former rival for Ann.

"Well—it's not nice to say things o' th' deyd," said John's mother's voice. "But I think tha're weel shut, Ann. He'd ne'er ha' done thee much good."

Which turned John into stone.

"Well, I'm beginnin' to think th' same," said Ann, sobbingly. "I made a mistake in takkin' him, an' if I'd my time to do again —"

Whereupon John leapt in amongst them, shouting and yelling like a lunatic, accusing their lack of human nature, and threatening to have the blood of Peter Dale, who only stood and grinned, from ear to ear. Whereupon John sat down and wept. The company went away.

"I didn't think tha'd start cheerin' thysel' up for my loss so soon," he said.

Ann wavered. Then she said: "It's gotten to be a reight good deyd mon as is bein' worth wed to, John."

And in that moment John realised his long shortcomings, and learnt the lesson they had intended him to learn by that scene, got up for his especial benefit, that he mustn't be too sure little Ann was going to go on standing that sort of thing.

For news had been brought to the village by a man who had met them in a pub the night before —and how they were coming by the first train in the morning.

As for Billy, he had to plead for himself, after all. But having 30s. left, it was not so hard.

In the parlour of John o' Bobs is a suite in old gold— bought out of the proceeds of the go-as-you-please — . It was often commented on that the singer-actor who appeared like a rocket had gone down like a stick, for he was never heard of again, though it is not forgotten—long ago as it is—and men who sat in the pit yet tell each other that the chap must have been drunk many a time to be able to act the thing like that.

Cotton Factory Times, April 2, 1920

Ruth's Burglar and the hidden money

Ruth watched her husband's figure pass along the sandy road, and out of sight. She had laughed when he asked her if she would be horribly nervous. All the savings of their six years of married life were in the house — six miserably skimped years of existence, during which she had looked at pretty things and bought none, but had toiled and schemed for this bigger life now opening to them. Ralph had bought the prettiest farm in the dale, with the richest land, and in one week they were moving in. Ho had paid fifty pounds of a deposit. The other five hundred was hidden snugly away.

"Rebecca will be here soon," thought Ruth, an hour after Ralph had called.

Despite herself she was feeling lonely. The fine rain had begun to blow. The sky was one dull grey. The garden was a sodden mass of dead autumn stuff.

And just then Ruth recalled her last night's dream, which until that moment had evaded her attempt to recall it.

Up the path came the postman. One letter — one only. She opened it as he closed the gate. The handwriting had yold her the purport of the letter. Rebecca could not come. But she read it through.

Then she put on her cloak. And, calling Jip, went off for a walk. But first of all she had a peep at the ten fifty pound notes.

It was half an hour later when she returned. The lonely feeling was in no wise walked off. Indeed, her nervousness was increased by the remembrance of a figure prowling about in the shadows of the wood, so that she had turned back, and, worst of all, lost Jip.

She made tea, whilst all the time she waited to hear that dear, doggy scratching at the old the door. But Jip did not return. Jip had not returned when the lamp was lit.

Someone knocked at the door, and came in without waiting to be asked.

"Oh!" said Ruth, in welcome.

It was Mrs. George from the cottage across the fields.

"I'm so glad," said Ruth. "I was feeling quite nervous." And she told the whole story of Ralph's departure, the money in the house, and Rebecca's failure to turn up.

"Eh, I'll send Biddy to sleep with you," said Mrs. George. Ruth could have blessed her.

At nine o'clock Biddy, a damsel of fourteen, came, carrying her nightdress with her.

"And mother says if you do get burglars, will you bang a tray at the window, and she'll get father up," said Biddy.

Ruth began to laugh. She had already laid her own plans to trap any enterprising burglar. Only one window in the house would not fasten.

"Come in here and see if this wouldn't scare any burglar, Biddy," said Ruth.

She led the girl into a semi-dark room upstairs. Biddy gave a piercing scream that ended in a laugh.

It took quite fifteen minutes to fasten up the house, and plant trays against every window, so that in the event of anyone trying to cut the pane out down would come the tray. Then — the money.

It was Biddy who said, "If I were you I'd put it in the coal hole, under a big cob of coal."

"You're a genius, Biddy," said Ruth.

It was certainly an unsafe place to leave five hundred pounds in a coal shed, without door. But as Biddy said, that was why it was so very safe.

Barricading the bedroom door with huge boxes, they finally retired to rest. For a long time Ruth could not sleep.

How long they slept they never knew. Bang! That was the sound that awakened them.

"Biddy! The tray's gone."

Biddy he began to shake, then to pray. Whilst Ruth, even in that moment, was vaguely surprised at herself. She did not scream, nor faint, nor call for help, as she had always imagined she would if ever a burglar came.

She remembered her promise to beat the tray. But quite

suddenly she was possessed with the fever to catch the burglar, and to catch him single-handed.

She crept out of bed and listened. There was no mistake about it, someone was fumbling about the door very cautiously, but she heard him.

Sho stole to the window and peered out. In the watery moonlight she saw the vague, mist-blotted outline of a man. He wore a bowler hat. The man in the wood had worn a bowler hat.

After some fumbling at the door, he finally went round to the back door.

Biddy was still praying.

"Biddy, he's going to climb up to the window where the ghost is," said Ruth.

And after a little while they heard him climbing up the out-house to reach that window. Then, after an eternity of agony to Ruth, she heard the sash of the window rattling in a sickening manner as it went up.

Then, indeed, Ruth wanted to scream.

The only hope was in the ghost—that horror she had manufactured out of her dressmaker's 'dummy'—that monstrosity with a starch-white face, on which were pinned black carricule eye-brows and eyes, and a black Kaiser William moustache!

Then—something flooded down inside the room. And Ruth knew he had tumbled in with the ghost. In the twinkling of an eye she had fastened the door on the outside. She had "got him". A great triumph throbbed through her.

"Biddy!" she said.

But Biddy had fainted.

"Let me out o' this. Let me out, I say!" said the man in the other room.

Ruth had no such intentions. She rushed to that window of her own room, and flinging up the window, began to beat a war-whoop on the tray.

"Let me out," pleaded the burglar.

The spell of the ghost was evidently upon him. Which Ruth did not wonder that. She had almost got afraid of the thing herself as she manufactured it. What surprised her was that he did not make his exit the way he had come.

Then another sound fell on her years. Someone was moving about outside. Then there must be two of them? Which almost made Ruth scream.

Then she remembered her signal. Help would soon be here.

Then she heard footsteps grinding on the coals, and dimly saw the flickering light of a match. She grew desperate. Under that big cob was five hundred pounds.

She flung up the window. "Who is there?" she enquired, in an over-loud voice. Stop him she must.

"Ruth!" said her husband's voice.

"Ralph!" she answered. She ran down in her nightdress.

"I tried to get back, thinking you'd be nervous," he said. "Missed the train. Thought you'd faint, thinking me a burglar, and decided to sleep on the coals for an hour or two."

"The five hundred is under that big cob," said Ruth. "And I've caught a burglar, Ralph."

She led him in, Ralph carrying the money, and, lamp in hand, they went upstairs. The door was now being beaten against in frantic terror. Whilst from outside came the murmur of voices, and help was near. "Open the door," said Ralph. He had listened intently to the voice.

"But he may be armed."

"Open it," said Ralph.

"If he—"

"Well, hold the lamp," in exasperation.

Ruth pulled back the catch. The door was opened.

Out tumbled a man, panic-stricken, almost raving, who calmed as he met Ralph's astonished gaze.

"Old man—no more wine—don't go in there—."

Ralph burst out laughing. "This is the man I bought the farm off," he told Ruth. "He's mistaken this house for his own. What's that?"

"The villagers," said Ruth, faintly. "I arranged to bang on a tray if—"

Upon the silence came the beating of trays, ostensibly to scare away the burglar.

Ralph met them at the door and explained. They were very disappointed.

As for Biddy, on their morning out, Ruth gave her a little silver watch as some compensation for her sufferings. And Ralph—Ralph never again told Ruth that if she met a burglar she would be paralysed. To his oft-repeated assertion that his was the bonniest wife in the universe, he added now the word "bravest". For, if she had not caught a burglar, it was certainly not her fault.

Cotton Factory Times, June 11, 1920

Courage, in two genders

She lay on her back in the tiny, unlovely bedroom, to which the sound of Mark's hammer, tapping the soles of the oldest shoes that walked Chippington, made a monotonous but not unpleasing sound. When the tapping ceased, and he brought up her dinner on a clothless tray, she said humbly, "Mark, when it's gone dusk tonight do you mind washing the front doorstep? The chapel folk'll pass tomorrow morning."

Mark's muddled glance met a coaxing one from the nicest eyes in Chippington.

"I'll not be taken for a molly," he said, irrately. "That's woman's work, Emily."

Mark was a conservative on these dividing lines between man's work and woman's. He clamped down five steps, then returned to the little room, and kissed his life clumsily. But both knew it as a confession of cowardice, and Emily Jay told herself fiercely that Billy Grimes, who was chapel organ blower, would hear that she was sick, and, noticing that dirty doorstep, believe her uncared for in her need. She did not, however, ask Mark again.

But a little coolness sprang up between them. It passed away in a few days, and neither was conscious of a recollection of it. Mark was busy in the shop, and Emily, with four children and spring cleaning, was kept busy as 'Trap's wife', when she got up.

Billy Grimes saw her in the street, and hoped she was better, and said she must never go short of anything she needed. He said he had known something was wrong that Sunday when the doorstep was not washed.

Billy always implied that Emily had made a big mistake in taking Mark instead of himself, whilst an irritable inner consciousness that Billy would have given her a hand in the house some time made Emily feel angry at Mark's attitude.

"I saw Billy today," said Emily, a little later. "I've no doubt he'd have cleaned that step for me."

Mark laughed.

"He's an old woman," he said. Then he added, "Do I asked thee to help me to mend shoes?"

Which was destined to come home to him, and the reply it brought forth.

"If I could lessen thy load by mending shoes I'd do it," said the little woman.

The idea of her hammering at Chippington's soles was too much for Mark. He pinched her ear and laughed again.

"At least I have the courage," flashed Emily. "Did Moses say a young woman shouldn't mend shoes? If he didn't, who cares, anyhow?"

Which surprised Mark.

Three days later he fell and broke his wrist. He had been run down for some time. The pain brought on a slight fever. Dazed and weak, he realised that for weeks he could not work. The new boot store was opening in Chippington. He had just cleared out the till to pay an old leather bill. They couldn't afford a man his wages. They were close now to the edge of the precipice on which it seemed they had been struggling all their married life.

The fever increased.

His mother came to nurse him.

Rocking by the side of a cup of tea, Emily Jay shed a tear or two, realizing the situation. Then the scheme to save Mark and Mark's business burst upon her like a flash, even while she wished.

She engaged a man for a week, and watched him closely whilst he worked, even helping him a little.

Then, on the stool worn shiny by the sick cobbler, sat Emily Jay, timidly defiant of what Chippington would think of her.

It was an ordeal.

Her first day was a nightmare.

The next day was bad, but rather less so, and the children round the window did not laugh so much. But it was hard at nightfall to know that Billy Grimes was watching her shadow hammering away, and to feel that she had lost caste.

A couple of pairs of shoes she heeled were brought back, nails having gone through.

But, slowly, and not very surely, she struggled on amidst a flood of boots, gradually getting mistress over hammer and awl.

She bound Mark's mother not to tell Mark.

"You're a brave lass," commented Mark's mother. "I couldn't have had the pluck to do man's work."

"I hate it," confessed Emily. "And when Mark finds out he owes the shop to my sitting on his stool — "

She burst into tears.

It was not the least part of her burden to know that Mark would possibly not forgive her for thus "letting him down".

On shop-closing day she went to Manchester, clad in her best. She was going to try and persuade Mark's dealer to allow them credit — a thing he had never allowed Mark, in the shoe line. Mark had never pressed. He always said it was no good. Mrs. Jay both pressed and smiled. She showed the advantage they would reap from using the house window to show off boots and shoes, and the prospect Chippington afforded. Mark's long, struggling business career had made him over prudent and pessimistic. Womanlike, Emily Jay took risks.

"Do you mean to say you are doing the repairing?" asked Mr. Dairs.

She laughed, tremulously.

"I think," she said, ruefully, "they're sending more repairs, because I'm a little slow."

A week later a consignment of holiday boots and shoes arrived in Chippington Station. Emily Jay turned her house window into a purple-curtained background for white shoes that appeared ready to trip away to sunlight and the sea. There were seashells and seaweed scattered among them.

The repairing became interfered with, on account of the fitting on of shoes.

She paid the bill within two weeks of contracting it and was promised more credit if she wanted it.

At the end of a month Mark agitated to come downstairs.

He believed a man's wages were running them to bankruptcy. They managed to keep him upstairs another six days. He came down on the Sabbath.

Both women were a little disturbed. Everything depended on how Mark took it. His wrist would not be fit to use for three weeks. Would his masculine pride forbid Emily to sit on that shiny stool doing his work? If so, the shop must close. The man who had worked for him for a week had enlisted. Labour was almost impossible to obtain.

Emily served him his breakfast of ham and eggs, and coffee in the blue willow pattern cups.

"Can we afford this?" he asked, with an invalid's moroseness.

Little John was standing on his buffet by his father, his eyes round and wide, his mouth daubed with egg.

"Mammy yammers," he said.

"Mammy what?" quoth Mark. He laid his fork down.

"Mammy — yammers — shoes," said Johnny, beginning to wobble a little.

"Have you been helping the man?" quoth Mark.

His tone scared the dear, loving woman looking helplessly at him across the table. In her agony she equivocated.

"He — he was a trifle slow," she said, almost hysterically. She was realizing that her courage was Mark's ignominy, even whilst she rebelled against it.

Old Mrs. Jay was shaking her head at Emily across the table.

"Mark," she said, seeing that the woman who had faced Chippington's opinion of a woman who hammered, was panic-stricken. "Mark, if it hadn't been for Emily tha'd have had no shop. They opened out at the corner a week after tha went down. Emily hasn't helped a man. She's been the man. She's kept thy place for thee."

Mark Jay regarded his mother with frowning brows. His utterance was thick.

"Do you mean to say — Emily has — " he began.

"She's worked till midnight every night," said Mrs. Jay, "an' now she wants her wages. And her wages are that she keeps this shop going till tha can take it on. Don't be a mean man, Mark Jay. She's the bravest last in Chippington."

Mark got up. He was struggling with himself. Then he said, dazedly, "I can hardly believe it".

"Show him," said Mrs. Jay.

Emily went into the shop. She sat down on the cobbler's tiny throne, and handled the hammer. The man with his arm in the sling walked into the place, and took up a pair of clumsy farmer's boots, and examined the mending of them.

"I couldn't have done them better myself," he said, grudgingly.

Mrs. Jay went to give the children the rest of their breakfast.

The man looked across at the little woman who had "yammered" the domestic boat into water-tightness. Something rose up and strangled his northern pride of sex superiority.

"Tha'rt the best little woman on the globe," he said, warmly. "An' to think I wouldn't clean that step for thee."

She took her wages with soft, feminine tears. They were all she had asked for.

Whilst in Chippington for ever after, when a man wanted to fix the date of an event, he would say, "before Emily Jay turned Mark's luck when he was sick there."

But it was noticeable that never again did she "yammer", though she attended to the women's and children's footwear. Which only proved to Mark of what calibre her courage had been.

When next she was sick, in the dim light the ghost-like figure of a man, stealthily cleaning the doorstep, was seen. Mark had crossed the boundaries of his fear into the land that is higher than sex — human service, done for a pal, who had stood by him.

Cotton Factory Times, July 23, 1920

Dick's Anconas: poultry and finance

When Dick Birch buried his grandfather, after paying all expenses he found he had £20 left.

"If tha doesn't mind tha'rt goin' to have gone through all that brass," said Mary chidingly, on the occasion of Dick's buying the children a spinning-top. "Tha'd go through a fortune."

"Nay, lass," expostulated Dick, mildly.

"If tha'd start something it would bring a bit o' extra money in an' keep th' capital safe, too."

Mary was turning the middle of a blanket to the sides, because it had worn thin.

"Eh, lass," said Dick, rather nettled; "it's not my fault we're poor."

"And I'm sure it's not mine," snapped Mary. "Anyhow, I were reading how some of them millionaires started life last week, an' they'd less nor £20. Will's a lot in this world."

Dick was mending Venetian blinds — one of the odd jobs he sometimes did to add ninepence to his wages. The three children were playing about the poxy kitchen. "I'll tell thee what I'll do," he said at length, "I'll start keepin' hens."

"Hens?" queried Mary. "I didn't know tha you knew owt about hens."

Dick winked.

"Hens runs in our family," he said. "Though this generation has been cooped up in factories, I believe I've a gift for poultry keepin'."

Mary pondered. "Well, don't let the grass grow under thy feet then," she advised. "Happen we've bin a bit too fleyd o' losin' ought to get on in the world." Which was rather comical, seeing they had never had anything to lose.

"That's it, lass. But we're going to make our fortunes now," said Dick. "Look at the price of eggs. We'll ha' to keep them hens on the intensive system."

Mary smiled. She looked bonny when she smiled, and Dick knew it.

"Tha'd have a job to keep them on th' extensive system," she said, "in a coal nook, in a yard joined at by four other families."

On the Saturday night following Dick arrived home at eleven o'clock with a crate of Anconas. He was quite drunk off three pints of beer, which he explained to Mary had cost him nothing. She got him upstairs, calling him divers names for 'beast' all the way up.

When she came downstairs she carried the crate of hens into the coal nook and locked them in. "Think on, tha thickhead," she told Dick on going to bed, "I've put them hens in th' nook."

"Aye, I'll 'member," said Dick.

Mary was awakened in the morning by a pandemonium of noise under the window. She thought it was either Long Will turning his wife out, or Jock, the fiddler, in the delirium tremens, or else that Nancy Allen, the consumptive young woman who lived alone, was dying.

She peeped through the hole in the lace curtains, and beheld an unforgettable sight. Dick, jacketless, was cautiously creeping on the top of the little row of coal-nooks belonging to the yard. On the very last of them, the nook belonging to Jane o' Betty's, stood an Ancona hen, regarding the man who was creeping towards her with a patient and wondering look. There were moments when Dick could have vowed the fowl winked.

Down below, watching the scene with deep interest, were some twenty spectators. The noise that had awakened Mary had subsided now. There was a great and dramatic hush on the yard. Some crisis was approaching.

"He's got it," acclaimed Jock the fiddler, who was in his shirt sleeves.

"Steady, Dick!"

This was Jane o' Betty's husband, the man with the finest homing pigeons for miles around.

"Grab her," came Nancy Ellen's voice, huskily, because she had a shawl over her mouth as a respirator.

Dick made a slight skilful movement nearer. The Ancona did not move. She regarded him in that gentle and inviting manner.

It was only as he touched her feather, the nearest to him, that she flapped her wings like a young eagle, and flew right over Dick's head.

It was his twenty-third attempt to catch her.

"Sitha, when I do catch thee, I'll ring thy neck," he said, tragically.

The sympathy of the spectators had gradually been merging into amusement. That remark was the turning of the tide. The yard broke into laughter, as though it were witnessing a pantomime with a good comedienne. All laughed with the exception of Nancy Ellen, the consumptive.

"You wouldn't laugh if it were your hen," she told Jock the fiddler.

At this moment Mary put up the window. Come in an' ha' your breakfast, Dick," she said.

It was the most sensible advice Dick had perceived that morning, but he was in too much a rage to heed it. For two hours he chased the Ancona, until even comedy palled, and the crowd faded away. Nancy Ellen still looked sympathy from her lonely window.

It was by throwing an onion bag over her from behind that Dick finally captured the Ancona. Nancy Ellen's door opened.

"Eh, I'm right fain tha's caught it, Dick," she said.

Ditka went in, after shutting up the hen. "Nancy Ellen's a daycent lass," he told Mary. "She'll not live long, poor beggar. She shall have an egg every morning—a brown 'un, off that Irish hen. As for them other laughing hyenas, I wouldn't sell 'em an egg for a pound-a-piece."

When he brought in the first egg, how Mary and the children gathered round to look at it!

"Eh, it's a grand 'un," said Mary.

"Fivepence-ha'penny there," he said.

"I believe there is money in it," said Mary.

"For thee, lass," said Dick. "Tha's worked hard."

Mary gazed from the egg to Dick. "I'm noan goin' to eat fivepence-ha'penny, "she said. "Give it th' child."

Dick stood looking at the egg on his palm. Then his face lit up. "We'll give it Nancy Allen," he said, in an inspired way. "Happen it'll bring us luck."

Mary beamed on him now. "I were just thinkin' the same myself," she said. "Dick, tha's a good heart, if tha'rt not worth a lot of brass." She kissed him, to Dick's astonishment.

"I'll take it in," said Mary, and took the egg in to Nancy Ellen.

"Eh, I'll pay you for it," she said.

Mary beamed and refused the money.

"They say brown eggs is the best," she remarked. "That motherly-looking Irish hen laid that. We've decided that hen is to lay just for thee, Nancy Ellen, so tha mun watch out, every morning, an' wait till it's laid, for thi breakfast."

Which did indeed become the one great event in Nancy Allen's day.

"There's something to do with this hen," said Dick, gloomily, bringing one in on a wet evening. They bedded it in the clothes basket, by the fire, sitting up half the night with it. At one o' clock it gave a weary gasp and made its escape, after having been treated for canker, roup, and for being egg-bound. They buried it in the yard.

"Live and larn," said Dick, "and will never say 'die'."

They did live and learn. On the next night he brought in another hen. Gloomily they sat up with it, expecting the passing forth. In the dim hours of the morning it laid an egg!

But the greatest excitement during Dick's spell of hen-keeping was when he caught Bella, the widow, with a hen-nest in her coal nook having beguiled the Irish hen to 'lay away'. Dick proved to her that she was not robbing him, but Nancy Ellen — whereupon she burst into tears, and promised never to do it again, but said she had been sending one to her daughter, who was just over confinement, and could not get eggs for love or money. Whereupon Dick gave her a dozen.

"If I were thee," said Mary, crossly, "I'd keep accounts. I don't think tha'rt making it pay."

"I don't see why we shouldn't eat 'em ourselves," said Dick. "We're as good as other folk. And we we work hard.

And we're dodgin' profiteers, an' that's better nor being one on 'em."

"Tha'll ne'er bi a Rockefeller," said Mary.

Dick sold out at the end of the year, save for one hen, which they called Nancy Allen's.

In the early spring Nancy Allen left a world of profiteering and profit years, dying in Mary's arms. She was conscious almost to the last.

"I don't think," she smiled faintly once, "Dick'll ha' lost a big lot on his hens, after a', Mary," she said. Mary thought her wandering.

"No. I'm sure it weren't much," she said.

"Lift Bridget for me to touch," said Nancy Allen.

Mary lifted up the buff Irish hen, with his soft, motherly look. Then tears dropped on its back.

"Tha's bin a friend to me," said Nancy Ellen, fondly.

A week later Dick and Mary learnt that Nancy Ellen had been in a club since she was a baby. After the funeral was over, they were left again with burying brass willed to them by Nancy Ellen.

"More Anconas?" asked Mary.

Dick stared at her. Since the rise in wages she had looked less harrassed, though if food galloped up after wages, that respite would not last long.

"Blackpool," he said, tersely. "It's years sin' I saw a bit o' yellow sand, and think of our Alice wadin' and shoutin', and Tom making castles, an' thee sat with a love tale in t' sand, wi' naught to do, and me smokin' an' looking at the water."

They went.

"Eh — if only Nancy Ellen could have been here, too!" said Dick, once. "It's a pity folk has to die for other folk to get a benefit. Lass — if I were a Rockefeller — "

Nancy looked at him over the top of the love-tale. There was a soft light in her eyes, woven then by sunlight and a sudden realization of Dick.

"Tha weren't cut out for one, Dick," she said. "And — I'm glad tha weren't." She laid a hand swiftly on his, and withdrew it as swiftly. They were forty, and the donkey man was coming.

Cotton Factory Times, November 12, 1920

www.ingramcontent.com/pod-product-compliance
Lightning Source LLC
Chambersburg PA
CBHW071436260626
47170CB00008B/2732